Jake

JACK WEYLAND

Deseret Book Company

Salt Lake City, Utah

Library of Congress Cataloging-in-Publication Data

Weyland, Jack, 1940–
  Jake / Jack Weyland.
    p.   cm.
  Summary: Vain, shallow television actor Jake Petrocelli has what he thinks is a near-death experience, which eventually causes him to reevaluate his life and join the Mormon Church.
  ISBN 1-57345-447-8 (hardcover)
  [1. Mormons—Fiction. 2. Conduct of life—Fiction.]   I. Title.
PZ7.W538Jak 1998
[Fic]—dc21   98-34551
                                              CIP
                                              AC

Printed in the United States of America

10 9 8 7 6 5 4 3 2 1   18961 - 6427

To Sherry, who has made my life a bit of heaven.

1

When Jake Petricelli was nineteen, he died. Or at least he thought he did. While he was dead, he fell in love with an angel. Not a real angel, of course. Andrea is good, but not that good.

Even so, something like that is bound to change your life.

* * * * *

Monday, June 15.

The lead story in the morning news was that the airline pilots' strike, now in its second day, showed no sign of ending. Talks had broken down the night before when company representatives walked out of a bargaining session. And the weather forecast called for another hot, muggy, summer day in Chicago.

Because *Wheels* was shot in a vacant warehouse with no air conditioning, the cast came early in the morning to avoid the heat. The locally produced television show was low-budget all the way. The cameraman was a fourteen-year-old boy who played video games between tapings, and a gum-chewing grandmother of one of the cast members held up hand-scrawled cue cards. The only thing of any real value on the set was a new Corvette, loaned for the day by a local dealer.

Muscular Jake Petricelli shut the hood of the Corvette and flexed as he tucked in his T-shirt. "Okay, that should about do it!" Jake played the part of Antonio, a darkly handsome auto mechanic with a slight European accent. He turned to face Melissa, a beautiful, wannabe actress he had found working at Wal-Mart a few weeks before. Like all of the girls Jake invited to play opposite him, Melissa was only too happy to be on *Wheels*. With his good looks and the newfound popularity of his television show, Jake had no trouble finding pretty young women to be on his show.

Melissa gave Jake an overdone drama-school hug. "Thank you, Antonio! Not only for fixing my car, but also for helping me to see I really can achieve my dream of being an Israeli fighter pilot!"

After wiping his hands on a shop rag, Jake, as Antonio, gave the smiling young woman a reassuring pat on the back. "Sure you can! You just start taking those flying lessons like we talked about." He turned to rummage through a stack of papers on his workbench. "I know I've got a bill here somewhere."

She came behind him, put her arms around his waist, and rested her head on his broad back. "I don't want to leave you," she pouted into the camera.

He turned to face her, draping his arms comfortably on her shoulders. "I think it's for the best though, don't you?"

"Why is it for the best, Antonio? Why?"

"Well, for one thing, I have to free up the stall, so I can get another car on the lift." He looked deeply into her heavily made-up eyes. "Brakes," he said in a husky voice.

She took the shop rag from him and used it to wipe a small grease smudge from his cheek. "How can I show my gratitude for all you've done to help me?"

"Hey, you already have, Tiger! Those donuts you brought were great."

She walked her fingertips up his bare arm and made a pouty face. "I'm going to miss you."

"I'll miss you too, seeing you in the waiting room, reading old magazines, and asking when's the last time I cleaned the place." He handed her the keys to her car. "But, hey, you're set now, so I'll be seeing you around."

She looked as though she were going to cry.

"Unless . . . " he said.

"Yes?" she asked, anxiously.

" . . . unless I do the 25,000-mile check-up." He paused as though thinking. "The only thing is . . . it'd be about 10,000 miles early."

She smiled and stood on tiptoe to throw her arms around his neck. "Oh, yes, Antonio! Please, do the 25,000-mile checkup!"

He smiled back at her. "Well, okay, but it might take a while. There's that brake job ahead of you."

She gave him a quick kiss on the cheek. "I don't care how long it takes! You know what? While I'm waiting, I'll go get us some more donuts!"

Melissa started to leave, then turned to face him. "You won't mind if I clean up a little when I get back, will you?"

"Maybe a little, but no drapes, you hear me? I hate drapes."

Too late. She'd already left.

Jake smiled to himself and rubbed his chin. Then, turning to the camera, he shook his head. "They always want to put up drapes."

Christopher Bergstrom, Jake's best friend from high school and the director of *Wheels*, called out, "And . . . out! Okay, that's it! Thanks, everybody. See you all in September!" He muttered privately to Jake, "If we can get somebody to bankroll us, that is."

3

Christopher was short, pale, and intense. The way things looked, in another five years he'd be totally bald. His life revolved around his clipboard and cell phone. The clipboard was stuffed with scraps of paper, some going back to junior high.

Christopher guided Jake past a group of female admirers, most of them in their teens, a few much older. "Sorry, but Jake can't talk to you today. He's got a train to catch."

"We love you!" one of the women called out.

Jake gave them all an insincere wave, then blew them a two-handed kiss. As Antonio, he called out, "I love you all, too! Thanks for your support!"

Jake and Christopher left the set and headed for Jake's dressing room. The warehouse where they shot the weekly sitcom was huge and desolate.

"Why are there so many losers hanging around here all the time?" Jake complained, dropping Antonio's accent and nice-guy image.

"They're your fans, for crying out loud. What do you want me to do, set up a barricade?"

"I suppose you're right. But why do they love me so much?"

"It's not you. It's Antonio they care about."

"How come?" Jake asked.

Since Christopher had created the character of Antonio, he spoke with conviction. "Because Antonio cares about other people, their hopes, their dreams, their sorrows."

Jake thought about it. "Naw—it's me."

Christopher scowled. "It's always you, right? Since first grade. You were always picked first for games. I was always chosen last."

"Yeah, but I was a lot better than you were."

Melissa caught up with them. "How'd I do, Jake?" she asked.

"Great, real good," Jake said, trying to be upbeat but bracing himself for what he knew was coming.

"I had so much fun! I'd love to do it again," she said enthusiastically.

Jake shook his head. "Look, you made a guest appearance, okay? And you did great. But what we mean by *guest appearance* is you don't come back."

Melissa's smile vanished. "I can change the color of my hair. Is it my weight? I can lose some more. Do you want me to be taller? I can do that. I can be Italian if you want. Would you want me to wear something more revealing next time? I can do that. Just tell me. I can be whatever you want. I'm very flexible that way." Her voice trailed off.

"We'll talk, okay?" Christopher said, taking Jake by the arm and pulling him away.

As they walked, Jake complained, "Sometimes I feel like every woman in Chicago thinks of me as an answer to her dreams."

"I know. It's crazy," Christopher said.

"Girls we've already had on the show keep calling me, begging me for another appearance. And then there's all the mothers sending me pictures of their daughters, wanting me to put 'em on. I've had five letters of proposal from complete strangers. And now there's Bernice. She wasn't here today, was she?"

"I don't think so."

"Good. She really scares me, Christopher."

"I know. Me too."

Bernice was a woman in her early forties who had been stalking Jake. Always wearing a belted raincoat, even in the heat of a Chicago summer, she had been hanging around the set of *Wheels*. Four times the previous week she'd come out of nowhere, from behind, always with the same intense stare and message. "Hello, Antonio. I'll always be here for you. You know that." She was obviously unstable, and Jake worried that if he made her angry, she might come at him with a gun or a knife. He had found being famous had its downside.

They entered Jake's dressing room. It had been thrown together with two-by-fours and plywood. Taped to the mirror were ads for sports cars and a few newspaper articles about the show. Jake removed the jeans and white T-shirt he wore on *Wheels*, then became distracted by his image in the mirror. Turning to admire the profile of his well-developed abs, he asked Christopher, "How much do you think they'd pay me to do a Hanes commercial?"

Christopher scowled. "For most people, being caught in public in their underwear is their worst nightmare. For you, it's a career move."

"I was just thinking about it, that's all." He stepped into a pair of cotton khaki pants, then worked on getting the makeup off his face. "While I'm in Seattle, I'm going to look around for a used Corvette. I've saved fifteen thousand dollars from *Wheels*. It's all right here." Jake waved a cashier's check in Christopher's face, then folded it and put it in his back pocket.

"This is not a shopping trip, okay?" Christopher lectured. "You do understand how important your meeting with Dwight Stone is, don't you?"

Jake noticed a blackhead on his nose. He leaned into the mirror to inspect it. "Relax, okay? I won't let you down. What do you do for blackheads?"

"I leave 'em—I need the color." Christopher shook the ballpoint pen he kept tied to the clipboard, trying to get it to write. "I can't believe I'm not going with you. Why did my sister have to pick tomorrow to get married?"

Jake's face was pressed to the mirror as he worked on the blackhead. "I'll take care of it. No problem."

"Doing underwear commercials may satisfy you, but I

want to win an Academy Award for best director some day. First things first."

Jake pulled on a short-sleeved, tight-fitting shirt that showed off his chest and arms. "You worry too much," he said, unzipping his gym bag and dropping a canister of Turbo Muscle Power into it.

Christopher retrieved a note he'd made earlier in the day. "Oh, there was a reporter here today from *People Magazine*. When I told her your schedule, she offered to take you to the station and interview you on the way."

"Another interview?" Jake complained. "Did you see what they wrote about me in the Sunday *Tribune*?"

Christopher shrugged. "Yeah, so? I thought it was okay."

Jake snatched a newspaper clipping from the mirror and began to read. "'In the locally produced sitcom, *Wheels*, Jake Petricelli plays the part of Antonio, the warm, sensitive friend every woman wishes she had.'"

Christopher smiled. "You see there? Some people do understand what Antonio is all about."

Jake continued to read. "'But in our interview, Petricelli came across as shallow and egotistical. Does America really need another third-rate actor slash mechanic?'"

Christopher suppressed a grin. "That's not true. You're a good mechanic." He noticed Jake's uneaten breakfast and went over to inspect it. He held up a bagel and small bottle of warm orange juice and looked at Jake, who nodded an okay.

"Do you think I'm shallow?" Jake asked.

Christopher cleared his throat. "Well, gosh, I don't know, I mean . . . "

"You do, don't you? Thanks a lot, Christopher."

"What can I say? You want to be in an underwear commercial."

"Let's just get out of here," Jake grumbled, grabbing his gym bag.

Christopher balanced the bagel, orange juice, clipboard, and cell phone as they left the dressing room and headed for the exit sign. "Last night when I talked to Dwight Stone, he said he'd give you five minutes, so talk fast."

They stepped out of the warehouse into the morning sun. There was a taxi waiting with its engine running. Off to the side, a gray, vintage Cadillac was parked near the door.

"That's your interview," Christopher said, pointing to the taxi.

"My mom's here. I asked her to take me to the station," Jake protested.

Christopher grabbed Jake's arm. "We really need the publicity. It's *People Magazine*! Look, call me after you've talked with Stone, okay? Don't let me down." Christopher gave his usual nod, then hurried back inside.

Jake's mom got out of the gray Cadillac.

Amelda Petricelli was short, tired, and street-smart. Sitting in the passenger seat, barely visible, was Natasha Salensky. Natasha had lived next door to Jake for as long as he could remember. They had played together as children. When they were six years old, their mothers had decided their kids should marry each other when they grew up. Jake was agreeable to the idea then, but not now.

Natasha had an olive complexion and a head full of straight black hair. She was also painfully shy. The main thing Jake held against her was that she was as sensible as his mother.

"We better hurry," his mom said. "Guess what? Natasha came along for the ride."

Jake took his mom off to the side. "Mom, you didn't tell me Natasha was coming."

"It's because she's got a big surprise for you today. She just got her braces off. Make her laugh. You won't be disappointed."

"I wish you'd quit trying to get us together."

"You could do a lot worse than her, believe me."

Jake glanced at his watch, and then at the taxi. The interview would be a way to escape his mom's meddling. He started to back away, toward the taxi.

"We're over here," his mom said.

"You won't need to take me to the station, after all. A reporter wants to interview me. *People Magazine.*"

His mom gave a sigh designed to lay a guilt trip on him. "Fine, if that's what you want."

"Sorry."

"What would be so wrong with marrying Natasha? She'd give you a large family. It's the hot gypsy blood in her."

"I know you mean well, but I really don't care for Natasha in that way."

"So? You didn't used to like liver and onions either."

"Mom, I still don't like liver and onions," Jake complained.

"But you eat it, and it's good for you, just like Natasha would be good for you."

"Not interested."

"Natasha fixed you something to eat on the train. I'll let her give it to you. Be nice to her, Jake."

Jake looked at his watch. "I'm in a hurry, Mom."

"Nobody is in that much of a hurry, believe me."

His mom went to the car and talked the reluctant Natasha into giving Jake the food. It was a hard sell, but finally Natasha emerged from the car carrying a wide-mouthed thermos.

Barely looking up, she handed him the thermos. "It's pigs in a blanket," she said softly.

Jake's mom gave an offstage prompt. "Smile, Natasha! Show Jake your teeth. Get your money's worth."

With great hesitation, Natasha managed a faint smile.

"Natasha, look," Jake said, "there's got to be somebody for you at the steel mill, okay?"

Natasha's smile faded.

Jake opened the door of the taxi. "And if that doesn't work, try league bowling."

Natasha was devastated, but Jake didn't care. He opened the door of the taxi, called out, "Bye, Mom," tossed his gym bag in on the floorboard, and got in. Already in the backseat, next to him, he discovered an attractive twenty-something brunette wearing a white blouse and, even in the heat, a navy blue business suit. Her dark brown hair was cut shorter than his and kind of spikey. Next to her sat a man wearing tattered jeans and a Chicago Bulls T-shirt. He was rumpled looking and hadn't shaved for a couple of days.

Extending her hand, the woman said, "Jake, I'm Tamra Carpenter, and this is my photographer, Carl Bradley. I understand you've got a train to catch. We'll get you there on time."

Jake sized Carl up. "You like pigs in a blanket?"

"Are you serious? I love the stuff!"

Jake handed him the thermos. "Be my guest. Compliments of Natasha Salensky."

Carl turned to get one last glimpse of Natasha, then opened the thermos and took a whiff. The smell invaded the cab and nearly made Jake and Tamra sick.

"Later, Carl," Tamra said. "We've got work to do."

They were now in heavy traffic, heading for the train station.

Tamra looked at her notes. "*Wheels* is the only TV daytime drama that takes place in an auto shop. How did that come about?"

Jake didn't even try to disguise his boredom. He'd told the story so often, he had it down pat. "When I was growing up, I was always hanging around my uncle's shop. When I graduated from high school, I started working there full time as a mechanic."

"No kidding?" Carl said. "I've got an '86 Ford that's been giving me a lot of trouble."

Tamra scowled. "Stow it, Carl!" Turning to Jake, she said with more interest, "Go ahead."

"Christopher Bergstrom and I grew up together. After high school, he started taking night classes in filmmaking."

"He's the director of *Wheels*, right?" Tamra asked.

Jake nodded. "He and I got the idea for *Wheels* one night at a bowling alley. We did one segment, took it around, and eventually got Channel 8 interested."

"Do you have any idea why *Wheels* is so popular in the Chicago area?" Tamra asked.

"Not really," Jake said in a tone of voice he hoped could be taken for humility.

"It's definitely not the plot," Tamra said. "It's always the same. A woman brings her sports car in to be fixed. She has a problem with her marriage, her family, or her career."

Carl butted in. "My car runs okay, but every once in a while it makes a noise, kind of like . . . ta-ta-ta-ta-boom . . . ta-ta-ta-ta-boom."

Tamra elbowed Carl to get him to shut up, then spoke to Jake. "In no time at all, Antonio fixes her car and her life. You show me a shop like that, and I'll change the oil in Carl's junker."

Carl sneered, "Now that I'd love to see."

"I can't explain why the show works," Jake said.

"It's simple," Tamra said, looking intently at Jake. "It's because of you. I'm told that women find you incredibly attractive."

Jake pretended to be hurt. "And you don't?"

Tamra smiled. "I can see why a woman could feel a certain . . . attraction," she said.

Carl, amazed, leaned forward to stare sideways at Tamra.

Tamra continued: "That dark brown hair, those brooding eyes, that outward toughness combined with a childlike vulnerability."

Carl snorted, slapping his knee for emphasis. "Don't mind her. She don't get out much."

Tamra whirled on him. "Not another word, Carl! Just sit there and reek of body odor. That's what you do best anyway."

* * * * *

Half an hour later, the taxi pulled up to the entrance of the train station. Tamra had the driver open the hood so she could have Carl take a picture of Jake pretending to work on the engine. Jake turned to face the camera and flexed his abs under his tight-fitting shirt as Carl snapped the picture.

By then it was almost time for his train to leave.

He grabbed his gym bag and said, "Thanks for the lift. I'd better go."

"Let me walk with you," Tamra said.

They hurried through the terminal and onto the platform. When they reached the train, Jake fumbled around in his bag, looking for his ticket. Tamra took advantage of the moment.

She said, "Jake, some day you're going to be a big star. I happen to think I'd make a great publicist for you."

Jake nodded. "Sure, let's talk about it when I get back in town."

She touched his arm. "If you want, we could talk about it on the train." She gave him a beguiling smile. "I've never been to Seattle before."

Jake shook his head. "I don't think so." He started to board the train.

"You'll call me when you get back in town?" Tamra called after him.

He shook his head. "Probably not."

She looked crushed. "Why not?"

"You want to be my publicist? Your problem is you want

it too much. The thing is, I don't respect that. I've got enough hangers-on around me now to last a lifetime."

Leaving her to stare after him, he turned and boarded the train.

As the train pulled out of the station, Jake found his sleeping compartment. He stowed his gym bag and then lay down on the bunk and fell asleep. He slept until two in the afternoon and woke up feeling restless and hungry. But he hesitated leaving the privacy of the sleeping car. He was tired of people, and he didn't want to take the chance of being recognized. The thought that Bernice, his stalker, might even be on the train passed briefly through his mind. But after spending half an hour pacing the cramped sleeping compartment, he finally decided to risk going out.

He found the dining car was closed until suppertime, so he decided to try the dome car.

As he slowly walked down the aisle of the dome car, looking for a seat, he did something he had begun doing when in a crowd: he watched for signs that anyone recognized him. Nobody seemed to. In a way, that made him feel better, but, at the same time, it also disappointed him.

He found two empty seats near the back of the dome car and sat by the window, watching fields of corn and soy beans pass by.

The train passed through a small town. *Maybe Dad is living here,* Jake thought. It was a game he played whenever he traveled. His dad had left home when Jake was twelve years old. Jake hadn't even known his parents weren't getting along. He came home from school one day, and his mom said, "Your father won't be coming around for a while."

"Why not?"

"He's got some things he needs to do."

"What kind of things?"

"I don't know. He doesn't want to be tied down anymore, so he's going away for a while."

That was all the explanation Jake could get from his mom, but he'd heard from others that his dad had run off with a waitress.

A frail, well-dressed elderly woman made her way down the aisle of the dome car. Stopping next to Jake, she asked, "Is this seat taken?"

"Not really."

She sat down. "Beautiful day, isn't it?" she said pleasantly.

"I suppose." Jake said distantly. He looked out the window, hoping to keep conversation to a minimum.

"Do you go to college?" the woman asked.

"No."

"What do you do?"

As he turned to face her, he noticed an expensive diamond ring on her finger. *If she's got money, maybe I can get her to invest in* Wheels, he thought. "I'm an actor," he said, flashing a sudden Antonio-like smile.

An hour later, the woman, whose name was Mrs. Undercott, was treating him as though he were her favorite grandson.

"Oh, sure, I admit that daytime drama has a bad reputation, but Antonio is the kind of friend every woman wishes she had," he said.

"Just like you then, right?" Mrs. Undercott asked.

"Well, I don't know about that," Jake said, feigning modesty. Then he asked, "Mrs. Undercott, how much do you think you could put up to help keep *Wheels* going another year?"

"Well, I don't know. I'm not much good with money. How much would you suggest?"

"Can I put you down for two hundred thousand dollars?"

"That sounds good."

Out of the corner of his eye, Jake caught sight of a conductor standing behind them in the aisle. He didn't know how long he'd been there. The man said, "Mrs. Undercott, there's a phone call for you. Would you like to take it in your sleeping quarters?"

Mrs. Undercott nodded. "Thank you, Mr. Montgomery." To Jake she said, "Excuse me, I'll be right back."

"After the call, you might like to take a nap," the conductor said.

"Perhaps so," Mrs. Undercott said. Montgomery gave a warning glance at Jake and whisked Mrs. Undercott away.

* * * * *

Jake waited until suppertime for Mrs. Undercott to return, but she never did, so he decided to look for her. He entered the crowded dining car.

A waiter approached. "Table for one?"

"I'll eat later. I'm looking for someone."

Jake searched all the passenger cars with no luck. Finally, an hour and a half later, he decided to check the sleeping cars. While passing through the train, he ran into the conductor Mrs. Undercott had called Montgomery.

"May I help you, sir?" Montgomery asked.

"I'm looking for Mrs. Undercott."

"She's retired for the evening, sir."

"Where is she staying?"

"I can't tell you that."

"Well, look, if she asks about me, I'll be eating supper."

"You're too late. The dining car is closed now."

"What? Not even a sandwich? I'm dying of hunger."

Montgomery hesitated. "I might be able to help you. Tell me where you're staying, and I'll bring you something in a few minutes."

Jake didn't feel as though Montgomery treated him with the respect he deserved, but went to his room anyway and waited for the conductor to bring him some food.

15

2

Andrea Warner was home for the summer, working as a lifeguard at the city swimming pool in West Glacier, Montana. In the fall she'd be returning to Ricks College for her sophomore year.

It was her first summer as a lifeguard. Swimming in chlorinated water was beginning to take its toll on her dark brown hair. It had gone frizzy and was dried out, and when she went home each night, she was tempted to cut it short. She also worried about being in the sun all day. For protection and for modesty, she wore a loose-fitting Ricks College T-shirt most of the time, but the shirt didn't cover her legs or face. She went through so much sunscreen she thought about buying it in gallon containers.

Andrea didn't know it, but she was the ultimate in understated beauty. Partly because she didn't want to attract the wrong kind of guy, but also because she didn't care a lot about clothes and makeup, she dressed simply. She was always more comfortable in jeans and a sweatshirt than in a dress. Her mother thought she ought to do more to fix herself up, but Andrea had grown up in the mountains of Montana and enjoyed being out-of-doors and active. It had given her a fresh, healthy appearance. So, although her beauty wasn't flashy, boys still found her attractive.

Late one afternoon, while keeping a careful watch on the swimmers in the water, she also carried on a conversation with Josh, a seventh grader and one of the regulars who came to the pool every day.

"Well, Josh, if you like Michelle, you have to show it by the way you treat her."

"How do I do that?" Josh asked.

"First thing is, be her friend. That's what a girl wants, someone she can talk to, someone who cares about her."

"I care about her."

"Then quit pushing her into the pool. Girls don't like that."

Josh looked confused. "How come?"

Andrea smiled at his lack of understanding. "Because she wants to be led into the pool by a nice boy like you," she said.

Josh smiled. "Thanks, Andrea, I'll try that tomorrow."

"You do that."

Just then Andrea noticed Mr. Stephenson from the city parks department coming out of the boys' dressing room. With his ample stomach cascading in multiple folds over the waistband of his swimming suit, he resembled a huge ocean liner leaving a narrow harbor. His pale skin had a chalky, almost gray look to it. Ignoring the giggling of some of the children, he came directly toward her. He had a huge beach towel draped over one shoulder.

"Mr. Stephenson, what a surprise! Are you here to swim?"

"No, I'm here to lifeguard. You should be with your family at a time like this. Why didn't you ask me for time off?"

"I didn't know who else could fill in. Besides, I don't mind. Sometimes it's better to keep busy."

"Go on, get out of here," he grumbled with an almost tender smile.

Andrea grabbed her things. "Thanks, Mr. Stephenson.

That's really nice of you. What about tomorrow? I can come in after the funeral."

Everyone in the pool stared with anticipation to see if Mr. Stephenson would make it up the ladder to the lifeguard station, and, if he did, if it would hold him without buckling.

Mr. Stephenson made the climb, then fought for breath. "It won't be necessary for you to come in tomorrow."

"How come? I know you've got other things to do. I could come at six so you can get home to your family."

Mr. Stephenson stared vacantly into the water. "I didn't want to have to tell you today."

"Tell me what?"

He sighed. "We didn't get the grant. We're going to have to close the pool for the rest of the summer. If only we hadn't spent so much on snow removal last winter."

"What if I work for free?"

"There are other expenses besides your salary. I'm sorry, Andrea, but we have no other choice. Besides, why would you offer to work for free?"

She shook her head and, glancing around the crowded pool at all the children, she said, "If the pool closes, what are all these kids going to do?"

* * * * *

After Andrea had showered and eaten supper, her mother, Marilyn Warner, asked Andrea to clean up Grampa's cabin. Andrea's cousin Cameron was coming for the funeral the next day and would be staying there.

Andrea rode her mountain bike to the cabin, which was nestled in the trees next to a small lake a mile or so from town.

When she opened the door of the cabin, a feeling of sadness washed over her. It was the first time she'd been there since her Grampa's death a few days before. For years, it had been a place she loved visiting. Grampa had always been there to delight her with his stories from the past as well as the lessons he'd learned that day from reading the scriptures, and to ask, with his characteristic warmth, how she was doing. As a young girl and young woman, whenever she had a problem, she had always gone to Grampa first, and then, if he suggested it, to her mom and dad. She and Grampa Reece shared a special closeness, and she had talked to him about things she never would have felt comfortable bringing up with her parents.

And now he was gone.

On a bulletin board, she noticed an old snapshot of her as a ten-year-old. In the picture she was standing next to Grampa Reece at Harrison Lake in Glacier National Park. She was proudly holding up a large cutthroat trout. In the background were snow-capped mountains.

The snapshot was bent and cracked, and Andrea carefully removed it from the bulletin board and put it in her shirt pocket.

While straightening up, she found an old photo album and sat down on Grampa's bed to look through it. The pictures reminded her of the many good times she and Grampa had spent together. He was the one who had taught her about the outdoors. They had gone rock climbing together and had explored the wilderness areas of Glacier Park. In the winter they had gone downhill and cross-country skiing. When she was fourteen, Grampa had given Andrea her first pair of snowshoes, and they'd spent hours tramping through trails that not even elk could make their way through.

While Andrea was reminiscing, a car pulled up. After a moment, Marilyn, Andrea's mother, came inside. "How you coming?" she asked.

Andrea closed the album and set it aside. "I haven't made much progress," she said.

"Too many memories?"

"Something like that."

"I know this is hard. I've got some time. Let me help you. I've brought some boxes. We need to donate some of his things to Salvation Army so somebody will get some use out of them. He'd want us to do that."

While Marilyn sorted through Grampa's clothes, Andrea made the bed with freshly laundered sheets.

"I'm really sorry about the pool closing," her mom said.

"I know, me too."

Marilyn found Grampa's old fishing hat. She plopped it on Andrea's head.

"I know he'd want you to have this."

Andrea took the floppy hat off her head and looked at it.

"What will you do for the rest of the summer?" Marilyn asked.

"I don't know. Right now I'm just going to try to get through the funeral, then I'll worry about everything else."

"You don't remember Cameron at all, do you?" Marilyn asked.

"Not really. Did I ever meet him?"

"Just once, when you were both about two years old. His parents came to visit, just before they moved to Boston. I have a picture of you two taking a bath together. You were both so cute."

"Mom, you're *not* thinking of showing that picture tomorrow, are you?"

Marilyn smiled. "It's tempting, but, no, I won't."

"What's Cameron like now?" Andrea asked.

"I'm not exactly sure. It's been so long. Your father and I saw him when he was twelve or so. He was a good-looking kid. Right now he's in college, studying to be an accountant."

"Is he a member of the Church?"

"He was baptized, but I think the whole family is inactive. I doubt if he knows very much about the Church."

It took them another half-hour to get the cabin ready for Cameron. On their way out, Andrea showed her mom the picture of her and Grampa on one of their many backpacking trips to Harrison Lake. "I don't know what I'm going to do without Grampa around," she said.

Her mother nodded. "He was a good dad for me, but, because he had more time when you came along, he was an even better grandfather."

After they got home, Andrea got into pajamas, read two chapters in the Book of Mormon, wrote in her journal, and worked for a little while on a home study course from BYU.

She was living a solitary life that summer. The non-member guys in her high school graduating class were mostly interested in girls they could party with. She'd long ago discouraged them about that. Nobody had called her to go out since she'd come home.

She'd met a few college students her age at the pool. Usually they were working at the park over the summer. One of them had asked her to go out with him after the pool closed and have a few drinks. She told him she didn't drink and instead invited him home to have ice cream and cookies with her family. A half hour later he left the pool with another girl.

Andrea was an only child. Her dad had been her grade school principal, and her mom worked as a secretary at the high school where Andrea attended. Vernon Warner was popular with the kids in his school. Every year he made a solemn promise to the children that if they would read a certain number of books, he'd kiss a pig or do something equally hilarious to children that age. And every year the children responded and waited anxiously for the day when he would keep his promise. They all thought they'd gotten the best of him. Until they grew up. And then they realized that he'd kissed a pig to give them a love of reading.

On the surface, Andrea's mother was efficient and competent, the kind of person who made the people she worked

21

for look good. But she had a tender side too. More students went in the office to talk to her about their problems than to the counselors hired for that purpose.

Andrea had enjoyed attending Ricks College the previous year. She'd made a lot of friends, and she especially enjoyed the members of her family home evening group. It wasn't going to be the same in the fall. Most of the guys she knew had left on missions after school let out in the spring.

Sitting on her bed, she reached for Grampa's fishing hat and put it on. She felt something in it and took it off and looked. A piece of notepaper was tucked into the sweatband. She took it out and unfolded it.

Andrea,

If you've found this note, then you already know about me leaving. Sorry about that. If it were up to me, my choice would be to live to see you married in the temple. But I guess I'll have to see that from the other side of the veil.

Could you do me a favor? The next time you go fishing at Harrison Lake, please retire this hat for me. I'd like you to cut it up into small pieces and throw the pieces to the wind. That way, part of me will always be there.

I love you very much. I'll be looking out for you as best I can from this side of the veil.

Love,

Grampa

Andrea got a pair of scissors, and, with tears in her eyes, carefully cut the old cloth hat into tiny squares. She put the pieces in a zip-lock bag so none of them would get lost.

"Oh, Grampa," she said softly, "I'm going to miss you so much."

* * * * *

On the train, Jake paced the floor in his small sleeping compartment, waiting for his food to show up. He'd only had a banana for breakfast and then had missed both lunch and supper.

Finally, there was a knock on the door. Jake opened it and there was Mr. Montgomery with a sandwich and a glass of milk on a tray. He came inside and set the tray down on a small table. "You mind if I stay here while you eat?"

"I guess not."

Montgomery sat down. "By this time of day I get a little tired of being on my feet."

Jake was so hungry that he picked up half the sandwich and stuffed the whole thing in his mouth.

Montgomery stared at him.

"I haven't eaten all day," Jake explained while chewing.

"I made the sandwich myself," Montgomery said. "It's ham and Swiss cheese with a little tangy mustard. If you slow down, you might even be able to taste it."

Jake rolled his eyes and snorted.

After a time, Montgomery said, "I'm curious. How much money did you think you could squeeze out of Mrs. Undercott?"

"I don't know what you're talking about."

"Oh, I think you do. I've been around a long time, and I've seen your type before. You're only in it for yourself, and you don't care who you hurt."

"Look, you've got me wrong, okay? I'm not some con artist trying to swindle old women. If she got into this, it'd be a sound business investment."

"Call it what you want, but there will come a day of reckoning when each of us will meet our maker. What will you do when you die?"

"Quit breathing?" He shoved the last of the sandwich into his mouth, wishing Montgomery would just leave.

But the conductor wasn't leaving. He apparently had something to say.

"At first there's darkness, and then a bright light coming

toward you," he said. He looked up as if he could see the light. "And then," he continued, "a family member, who's already died, comes to escort you to where you will spend the rest of eternity."

Jake nodded his head in mock agreement. "Well, that's something to think about, all right." He dropped a twenty-dollar bill on the tray and handed it to Montgomery.

"Thank you, sir. Do yourself a favor and think about this while there's still time."

"Yeah, sure." Jake shut the door, gave a sigh of relief, and found solace by watching a movie.

* * * * *

Later that night, Jake tried to sleep, but it was no use. One thought kept coming to mind: Once he arrived in Seattle, he'd lose his chance to get Mrs. Undercott to come up with some money for *Wheels*.

At three in the morning he got out of bed and got dressed. He knew, from having lived with his grandmother for a month after his folks got divorced, that old people don't sleep very well at night. Maybe Mrs. Undercott would be awake in her sleeping compartment, and all it'd take would be for him to knock on her door. She'd let him in, they'd talk for a few minutes, and then he'd leave with a check for two hundred thousand dollars.

It was a good enough reason to lose a little sleep.

He slid his cell phone into the pocket of his light jacket in case Mrs. Undercott had some questions about *Wheels* that Christopher would need to answer.

He went from door to door, knocking quietly enough so if someone was asleep it wouldn't wake them up, but some-one still awake would hear the knock.

Outside one of the doors he saw a tray of half-eaten food. Jake was still hungry. He knelt down and sorted through what was there. He found a half-eaten roll. He wiped it over the dried-out sauce on one of the plates and devoured it.

He knocked on the next door and was startled when a giant of a man immediately flung the door open.

"What do you want?" the man demanded.

Jake looked at his key. "Oh, gosh, this isn't my room, is it? Sorry."

"Here, maybe this will help you remember," the man said, shoving Jake backward into the wall. "Don't let me catch you around here again."

Jake had had enough. He decided to try and get some sleep.

As he headed to the next car, where his sleeping compartment was located, the train began to slow down. When he was in the space between the two cars, he looked out a window. They were coming into some kind of town. Jake saw a GAS/FOOD sign glowing in the night. If the train was stopping he might be able to run to the store, get some food, and get back on the train before it left.

As soon as the train stopped, Jake jumped down from the car and began running toward the GAS/FOOD sign. The last thing he needed was to have the train pull out without him, so, to save time, while still running, he got his wallet out of his pocket. He fumbled through his cash, looking for a twenty-dollar bill he knew was there somewhere with the fifties. Unfortunately, he ran head-on into a wooden signpost and fell to the ground unconscious.

* * * * *

He had no idea how long he lay there, but when he came to, in the darkness he saw a bright light coming toward him. Jake grabbed the cell phone, and hit recall. "Christopher, Christopher, can you hear me?"

25

No answer.

"Christopher!"

The phone was dead.

"I'm not ready to die!"

It made no difference. The light continued to advance toward him. And then it was on top of him. Jake passed out, and his cell phone rolled down a ravine and landed in the weeds.

3

At quarter-to-nine in the morning, wearing her usual jeans and a sweatshirt, Andrea came into the kitchen where her mom was peeling potatoes for the family luncheon at the church after the funeral.

"I'm going to get Cameron now. And then I'll go practice at the church with Sister Nielson."

"If you're going to practice in the chapel, I think you should wear a dress. Maybe that one you wore on Sunday."

Andrea thought about objecting to the idea of changing, but, because her mom made few such requests, she didn't. From her mom's puffy eyes, Andrea could tell she'd been crying. "You okay, Mom?"

"I just need a hug, that's all."

Andrea gave her mom a big hug. "If there's anything you need me to do for you today, just ask, okay? Anything at all."

Marilyn kissed her on the forehead. "How did I get so lucky to have you for my daughter?"

"I'm the lucky one."

"I've been thinking about you," Marilyn said. "Now that the pool is closed, maybe you should think about moving to Seattle. You could live with Hal and Shirley and maybe get yourself a good job."

"I'd rather stay here for the summer."

"With Ben gone, there's nobody here for you anymore." Ben had been the only member of the Church in her graduating class. He had been called to serve a mission in Russia, and was now in the MTC.

"It's okay—there's going to be so many cute guys at Ricks next fall. Besides, I'm in no hurry." She looked at the clock. "Well, then again, maybe I am. I'd better get going. I'll change and then get Cameron. It's such a nice day, I think I'll walk."

* * * * *

Jake was still lying in the weeds near the train station platform. There was no telling how long he might have slept, but, at 9:45, a passenger train began pulling out of the station. The noise woke him up, and he struggled to a standing position just as the end of the train moved by in front of him.

With the train gone, he looked across the tracks to the station platform. There stood the most beautiful girl he had ever seen. Back-lighted by the sun, she had long brown hair with auburn highlights and was wearing an elegant, creamy-white, long dress. What struck him most, though, was that she appeared to be waiting for someone.

Jake knew what that meant. He had experienced the darkness; he had seen the oncoming light. His time on earth was over, and this beautiful creature had come to escort him to the afterlife.

He was a little fuzzyheaded still, and it seemed strange to him that his head hurt. There was also a big bump on his forehead. He had always thought that when you died, all your aches and pains would go away. That didn't seem to be the case, but, of course, he'd never paid much attention to things like that. Maybe the priest had talked about it the few times Jake had gone to mass, and he'd just missed it.

The two of them walked slowly toward each other, and she gave him a friendly smile.

"Have you come to show me the way?" he asked.

"Yes, I'm your cousin Andrea. We've been expecting you."

Her enthusiasm about him dying depressed him. "So . . . it's all over then, right? I really wasn't prepared . . . for this . . . but I suppose no one ever is."

She nodded. "Yes, it came unexpectedly . . . for all of us."

"For you too?" he asked.

"Oh, yes."

"I'm so sorry," he said. "You're so young."

"I'm nineteen," she said.

"Same as me. Still though, that's too young . . . for this." He sat on the bench in front of the station to collect his thoughts. He buried his face in his hands.

She sat beside him and touched the sleeve of his jacket. "Are you okay?"

He sat up. "Sorry, it's just that . . . I can't believe this has happened."

"I know. It's been hard on all of us."

"There's so many things rushing through my mind. Things I've never thought about before. Like my mom . . . I miss her already."

Andrea put her hand on his shoulder. "How long has it been since you saw her?"

"I saw her yesterday. I . . . " He couldn't finish the sentence. She fished a tissue out of her pocket, and he used it to blow his nose and wipe his tears. "Sorry."

"No, that's fine. I think it's great you feel so close to your mom. Not many guys your age do, you know."

He wiped his eyes. "I never thanked her for all she did for me."

"That is so sweet," Andrea said softly.

"She always made me liver and onions," Jake blurted out.

"Really? Is that one of your favorite foods?"

"No, I hated it." He fought back the tears. "But maybe if I'd just tried a little harder . . . " With that, he completely lost it.

She patted him on the shoulder. "It's okay. I don't like liver and onions either."

He felt self-conscious breaking down in front of her. *It's time to face this like a man,* he thought. He wiped his tears and stood up.

"Are you ready to go now?" she asked.

"Yes, of course." He let out a deep sigh. "I know you've come to help me."

"Do you have any luggage?"

Jake was surprised she would even ask. "No. Mom used to say, 'You can't take it with you.'"

Andrea nodded. "I know what you mean. I had my bags lost once too. Well, let's go."

They walked together down the sidewalk of a residential street. To Jake, it felt like morning, and the air smelled fresh and clean.

"So what do you think of our little town?" she asked.

"Well, it's okay, but, actually, I'd imagined it being different."

"In what way?" she asked.

"Oh, I don't know, more *heavenly,* I guess."

She smiled. "It's a nice enough place. I like it anyway."

"No, it's fine, really. I mean, who am I to complain? It's just like a small town in . . . "

"Montana," she suggested.

Jake looked around, thought about it, then nodded. "Sure, why not? It could be Montana. It's a nice touch, really, when you think about it. For one thing, it's not scary, you know what I mean? But, of course, I'm sure it was designed that way."

She seemed a little confused. "Maybe so."

As they passed a white house on the corner, a woman came out. "Good morning, Andrea. Who's your friend?"

"This is my cousin Cameron."

Jake cleared his throat and said quietly, "Actually, most people call me Jake."

"Sorry," Andrea said to Jake and then explained to the woman at the door, "he goes by Jake now. We haven't seen each other since we were about two years old. He's from back East."

"Nice to meet you, Jake. I'm Sister Nielson."

"Nice to be here . . . well, not really, but I'll try to make the best of it."

"Good for you, dear," Sister Nielson said, then continued, "Andrea, I was just about to call you. My day is getting more complicated by the minute. Instead of practicing at the church, could we just run through your song now?"

"Sure, no problem." She turned to Jake. "I'm sorry—do you mind?"

Jake shrugged his shoulders. "No, go ahead. I have all the time in the world . . . now."

They went inside. Jake sat on the couch while Andrea and Sister Nielson practiced at the piano.

Ordinarily Jake was not an emotional person, but, being so recently dead, he couldn't help himself, especially with Andrea singing "Amazing Grace." Her singing voice struck him as, well, angelic. By the time she finished the song, he was wiping his tears on a couch pillow.

Sister Nielson turned on the piano bench and saw what he was doing to her pillow. "There are some tissues in the bathroom, dear."

Jake stood up, stunned at the news. "You have . . . bathrooms . . . here?"

Mrs. Nielson glanced at Andrea, then answered, "Why, yes, we do."

"That is so *amazing!* Who would ever think there'd be bathrooms here, you know what I mean?"

Mrs. Nielson glanced at Andrea and whispered, "Is he okay?"

"It was a long trip—he probably didn't get much sleep."

As Jake stepped into the bathroom, he heard Mrs. Nielson say to Andrea, "Easterners—they come here expecting us to still be living in covered wagons."

A few minutes later Andrea and Jake were on their way again. They were quickly out of town, walking along a seldom-used road.

He didn't want to be impolite, but he was fascinated with Andrea, partly because of her beauty, but, also, because he kept looking for clues of what it meant to be dead.

She was only an inch or two shorter than he was. It surprised him that she was so tan because it was hard to imagine angels in tanning booths. He wondered if it was a bonus you got if you'd lived an especially good life.

Her hair, long and dark brown, was pulled back off her face, and she wore a gold clip on top of her head. He liked seeing all of her forehead; it made the front-view shape of her face almost a perfect triangle. Her eyes were unusual. The dark brown pupils were large and flecked with little green spots.

It made her uncomfortable to have him study her so intently. "Anything wrong?" she asked.

"No," he stammered. It's just . . . I don't know what to think . . . I mean, I've never seen an angel."

She grinned. "You really *didn't* get much sleep last night, did you? Well, I hope you can work in a nap because we have a big day ahead of us."

"We do?"

"Yes. The funeral is today," Andrea said.

"So soon? There must be some kind of a time warp here, right?"

"I wouldn't know about that, but the funeral *is* today."

"Can I be at the funeral?" he asked.

They turned onto a small path that wound its way through the trees.

"Of course. You think we'd let you come this far and then tell you that you couldn't go to it?"

"I'm glad I get to be there, even though I know that nobody will be able to see me."

"You don't want anyone to see you?" she asked.

He shook his head. "I don't want to scare anybody."

Andrea patted him on the back. "Hey, relax, okay? You're with family now."

"Sorry. I just don't know what's expected of me here, that's all."

There was much he found fascinating about her. When she smiled, a tiny dimple magically appeared on the lower part of her left cheek. It was like her face's gift to anyone who might brighten her day.

They came to a small meadow covered by a dense blanket of delicate wild purple flowers. Andrea stopped to pick a few.

"Look, I know it's kind of late to be asking this, but is there a God?" Jake asked.

Andrea handed him the bouquet she'd picked. "What do you think?"

Jake took in the delicate beauty of the flowers. "There is then, right?"

"Of course."

Jake sighed. "I've always wondered. Okay, so now I know."

Andrea searched his eyes. "You believe me?"

"Why wouldn't I believe you? You should know, right?"

She gazed into his eyes. "I do know, Jake."

"Of course you do. So now I know too."

They came to a pond covered with water lilies. They could hear the occasional sound of frogs croaking.

"Most guys are too proud to just accept it if I tell them there's a God."

"I'll believe whatever you tell me."

"You trust me that much?" she asked.

"Of course. Go ahead, teach me all I need to know."

She seemed confused. "All you need to know for what?"

"So I can be more . . . well, like you."

"You want to be like me?" she asked.

"Sure. Don't most guys who come here tell you that?"

She smiled. "So far you're the only one." She tossed a small rock into the pond, setting off more croaking by the frogs. "Not every frog a girl makes friends with is a prince. Some really are frogs." She sighed. "In fact, most of 'em."

"Really?"

"With one exception. His name is Ben. We were friends in high school, but now he's in the empty sea."

At least that's how it sounded to Jake. He could imagine what it meant. A person in an empty sea would be alone and without hope. He'd felt that way himself many times.

"When guys come here, why don't they try to learn from you?" Jake asked.

"They're probably afraid it will take away from their masculinity. But, for me, it'd only make me respect them more."

"I'm glad you were the one who came for me. I feel better just being with you."

"Actually, I feel the same way. Strange, isn't it?"

They stopped walking and gazed into each other's eyes. It didn't last long though, because she thought he was her cousin, and he was convinced she was an angel. So their brief eye contact ended up making them both feel guilty.

Andrea was the first to turn away. Her face was a bright red. "It's probably because we're cousins," she said.

A short time later they came to Grampa's cabin. It sat on

34

the shore of a small lake and in the background stood a towering, snow-covered mountain peak.

"Well, we're here. This is where you'll be staying," she said.

Jake wasn't sure if this was heaven or hell, but, either way, it did have a nice view. "Will I like it here?"

"I don't know. Some people don't, but I do."

He found that reassuring and nodded gratefully. "If you like it, I will too."

They went in and looked around. "Well, this is it. It's not much, but it's homey." She showed him where an extra blanket was stored in the closet, in case it got cold during the night.

"So this is where I'll be staying?" He gave a troubled sigh.

"For as long as you're here," she said.

Looking around at the interior of the small cabin, Jake said, "Actually, this is way more than I deserve."

"Don't be down on yourself, okay?" She opened the cupboards. "One bad thing, though, there's not much food here."

He shook his head. "I'm sure that'll be the last thing on my mind." Even though he was experiencing something that resembled hunger pains, he didn't want to admit it, thinking it was a weakness that he'd get over eventually.

"You're fasting until after the funeral? I've got to tell you, I'm really touched by that. Let's go sit out front and talk."

They sat on two homemade rocking chairs fashioned from willow branches. Jake was fascinated with the tallest mountain peak in the distance. "Does God live up there?"

She nodded. "I've often thought so."

"What will happen after the funeral?" he asked.

"Well, that's pretty much up to you," she said. "What do you want to happen?"

Jake began to rock in unison with her. "I want to stay

with you for as long as I can. What will you do today after everything's over?"

"Probably go home," she said.

Jake, thinking that's where heaven was, looked up at the highest peak. "You call it . . . Home . . . then, right? I like that. That's where I want to go after the funeral . . . Home . . . with you."

She cleared her throat. "Well, I guess that'd be all right . . . at least for a while."

"How long could I stay with you . . . at Home?"

"Well, I don't know," she said, clearing her throat. "How long were you thinking of?"

"For as long as you'll let me."

"For more than a week?" she asked.

He chuckled. "Oh yeah, *much* more than a week."

She seemed worried. "Well, I don't know. I mean, after a while, it might get . . . well . . . crowded."

Jake gazed at the snow-covered peak. "It gets crowded there . . . at Home?" he asked.

"Well, it hasn't yet, but it could."

Jake was grateful to be learning so much about the afterlife. "I didn't know that."

She stood up. "Look, I should probably go so you can rest up."

"Not yet. There's so much you can teach me."

"You keep saying that. What exactly do you want to know?"

"I want to learn about Life and Death and Home."

She studied his face. "You really want to know about those things?"

"Oh, yeah, now more than ever."

"I guess I could stay a little longer then."

"Is there some place you go around here when you need to think?" he asked.

She pointed to a rocky outcrop on the mountain. "Up there."

* * * * *

Just past the lake, the trail started to climb. After walking a while, they came to a shady place where the trail was blocked by a hundred-foot section of snow. As they made their way over the crusty snow, she turned and gently tossed a handful at him. It hit him in the face. She started giggling and ran away, expecting him to chase her.

Thinking this was punishment for his sins, he made no effort to stop her.

"Sorry about that," she teased.

"It's okay, really," he said.

She tossed more snow in his face. He lowered his head and endured it.

"Don't you want to throw some snow at me?" she asked.

"No, but you go right ahead. If you'd like, I can lie down in the snow. Then you can just kick it in my face. That way you won't get your hands cold."

Andrea's smile faded. "I don't want to hurt you, Jake. I just thought it'd be fun to have a snowball fight."

"Oh, I could never throw snow at you."

"Why not?"

"I have too much respect for you to ever do anything like that."

Andrea dropped the snowball. "Gosh, I feel really bad now."

"Really, it's okay. Don't worry about it."

Once again, they found themselves gazing into each other's eyes. "You are the gentlest, most sensitive guy I've ever met," she said, shaking her head.

"I wish that were true. Maybe I will be someday, though, if I can spend enough time with you."

37

They continued their climb, and a few minutes later they made it to the overlook. "Now I know why I don't usually hike in a dress," Andrea said, pulling stickers from her dress.

Jake stepped to the edge and looked around. He could see mountains, lakes, meadows, and across the way, a thunderstorm moving in. "It's amazing how you can be alive one minute and then dead the next."

"I know what you mean. Grampa was so active until the last, and then one day he just . . . up and died."

"Is Grampa here now?" he asked.

Her lower lip began to quiver. "You know, I think he is. Grampa was the one who first took me up here. I'd forgotten that. Yes, you're right. Grampa *is* here with us."

"I figured he was. Either here or . . . at Home." He glanced up at the highest peak.

"You're amazing," she said. "You have so much insight."

"Not really. But you've been a real comfort to me."

"Glad to help out." She held both his hands in hers for just a second.

"I don't really know how things work, and I hope you won't be offended, but if I could have anything I wished for, it would be to be with you forever."

She cleared her throat and stared at him. "Why would you want that?"

"So I can learn as much as I can from you."

She was deeply touched by his comment. "That is so amazing."

"What?"

"All my life I've dreamed of having someone I could share my thoughts, ideas, and dreams with."

"Please do that with me." Jake reached out to touch her hand, but then pulled back because he wasn't sure that was allowed. "Before you came . . . here, what was your life like?" he asked.

"Well, up until yesterday, I was working at a local swimming pool as a lifeguard."

"You were working at a swimming pool yesterday, and yet today . . . well . . . you're Home?"

"Yes, that's right."

He wanted to know how she'd died. "What happened?"

"Well, the city ran out of funds so they had to close the pool. I felt so bad when they told me."

"So you . . . went . . . Home . . . right after you found out about the pool closing, is that right?"

"Yeah, that's right. Why do you ask?"

He patted her hand. "I'm not sure how to say this . . . but did things seem so hopeless yesterday that you took it into your own hands . . . to get you Home?"

Andrea nodded. "I rode my bike."

What a horrible way to die, Jake thought. "Over a cliff?"

She seemed confused. "Why would you even ask a question like that?"

He nodded. "You're right. It's none of my business. Sorry."

Jake liked it best when she looked at the mountains or the lake or the dark clouds moving in, because that was when he could gaze freely at her. She wore little, if any, makeup. Because he'd spent the last year surrounded by girls whose faces were almost an entire marketing campaign, it was refreshing to look at Andrea.

He suspected she actually had two dimples. The one on the left showed up with the slightest smile. He had not yet seen the one on the right, but he still thought there might be one there. If he could only get her really laughing.

"I feel so bad for the kids in this town," she said. "There's practically nothing for them to do. And now with the pool closed . . . "

"If I'd known earlier, I could've helped. But it's too late now."

"How could you have helped?" she asked.

"Before I came . . . here, I could've given some money to keep the pool open."

"I'm afraid it would have taken more than a few dollars."

"How much?"

"Well, I'm not exactly sure, but I'd guess several thousand dollars."

"That would've been no problem. But it's too late now."

"Why is it too late?"

Jake pulled the folded-up cashier's check from his pocket and handed it to Andrea. "Too bad this is no good here."

She examined the cashier's check. "Well, it is from an out-of-state bank, but it's a cashier's check, so I don't think that'd be much of a problem."

He shrugged his shoulders. "Sure, why not? I was saving up for a Corvette, but I have no use for that now. Go ahead, keep it."

"You can't be serious. This is for fifteen thousand dollars!"

He shook it off. "Yeah, so? It's just money, right?"

Andrea stared at the check in disbelief. Then her eyes got misty. "This is the nicest thing anyone has ever done for me. Not just for me, but for all the kids in town."

He tossed it off. "I'm just glad it'll do some good."

She gave him a big hug and kissed him on the cheek. "You are such a wonderful guy!"

He was nearly overcome. "I never thought I'd be kissed by an angel."

"You are so kind and decent." She started to blush. "There's something else about you. It's kind of embarrassing to admit, but . . . I really like looking at you."

Jake nodded matter-of-factly. "Yeah, I know. I used to love that too. Here, let me show you something." He lifted his shirt and, guilt-ridden, confessed, "I wasted so much time working on my abs—time I could have spent working in a homeless shelter. You know what? I wish I'd met you before I came here."

"Why?"

"With you as my example, I could've turned my life around. Everything is so clear to me now."

"You're fine just the way you are," she said, moving closer to him. "How come I've never met a guy like you before?"

He sighed. "You're the special one, not me. The world is full of guys like me . . . arrogant . . . shallow . . . "

She put her finger on his lips. "Don't talk like that. I think you're wonderful."

He shook his head. "I wish I were." He sighed. "I wish I had been."

They stared into each other's eyes, and the distance between their lips began to slowly close. Andrea closed her eyes and tilted her head slightly.

They were about to kiss when a flash of lightning and the clap of thunder put the fear of everlasting punishment into Jake. He jumped away from her. "Is this some kind of a test?" he blurted out, afraid he was about to be struck by lightning.

Andrea, her face flushed, also moved away. "You're right. My gosh, what were we thinking? I am *so* embarrassed." She looked at her watch. "It's getting late. We'd better start back."

Jake led the way as they started back down the trail. "I'm really sorry about . . . you know . . . what almost happened back there."

"Yeah, me too. Let's just forget about it."

"I hope it doesn't change things between us," he said.

"Of course not. Cousins can be best friends."

He turned to face her and walked backward as they talked. "Will the fact that we're both dead be a problem for us?" he asked.

After a long pause, she said, "I assume you mean that in

the sense . . . that most of us are dead to what's really important in life."

"No, I meant it in the sense that . . . we're both . . . dead."

"I'm sorry. I still don't understand."

Still walking backward, Jake stumbled on a rock and lost his balance. As he fell, he tried to stop himself by catching hold of a tree on the edge of the trail. Unfortunately, the tree was rotten and gave way.

So Jake ended up falling off a cliff.

4

Fortunately, Jake landed in a thicket of prickly bushes, which tore his skin but cushioned his fall.

"Jake? Are you okay?" Andrea called out. She was standing on the edge of the cliff, about fifteen feet above him, looking down at him. He was lying face-up on the bush he'd crushed when he landed.

How can this hurt so much if I'm already dead? he thought. His attention was drawn to a cut on his leg. "I'm bleeding."

"Is it very bad?"

"Not really. It's just that after meeting you, I didn't think I'd ever bleed again."

There was a long pause. "Did you hit your head too?"

"No."

"Okay, good. Look, I'm coming down. It might take a while because I'm going to have to backtrack, but I'll come as fast as I can. Just try to rest, okay?" With that, she disappeared from view.

He struggled to get himself untangled from the bush. "Andrea, is this hell? Because if it is, I think you should at least have the decency to tell me."

No answer.

"This whole place is booby-trapped, isn't it?" he called

out, but this time his voice was weak. He felt his strength ebbing away.

"Did you say something, Jake?" she called from some place above him.

"Never mind."

By the time he got himself untangled from the bush, he was exhausted. He lay on his back trying to catch his breath. When Andrea arrived, she took one look at him and said, "Oh, my gosh, you poor guy."

The first thing she did was examine his cut. "This doesn't look too bad." She tore off a small strip of cloth from the bottom of her dress and used it as a bandage.

She had a gentle touch and yet seemed to know what she was doing. Watching her helped him make up his mind. *This can't be hell. Not with Andrea here.*

She avoided eye contact until she was done, and then, with a smile, she asked, "Why do you keep staring at me?"

"I've never met anyone like you before." He shook his head. "That was dumb, wasn't it? Of course I haven't."

He held her hand. "I can see things so clearly now. I know where I went wrong. Before I came here, it was always me, me, me, with never any thought for anyone else. Is there still time for me to change? I mean, here?"

"Sure, Jake, you can always change."

He gave a sigh of relief. "I will then. You'll see."

"We can talk about this later, but right now let me go get Search and Rescue to come and haul you out of here."

Jake was, once again, confused. "You have Search and Rescue . . . here?"

"Oh, sure, there's always somebody coming out here and getting lost."

"Why do you need Search and Rescue here? I mean, if you people can't keep track of newcomers, who can?"

She gently put her hand on his forehead. "Take it easy, Jake."

Jake shook her off, sat up, and looked around. "And if this is hell, why do you even care if somebody gets lost? I mean, that's why they call it hell, right?"

"Jake, *please,* calm down, okay? I'll go get Search and Rescue. I won't be long." She stood up to leave. "The most important thing is you're still alive."

"I am?"

She smiled. "At least you haven't lost your sense of humor." She started to walk away.

"Wait, don't go yet."

"What's wrong?" she asked.

"I think I might have a little amnesia. Could you fill me in on everything that's happened today?"

"Well, I met you at the train station," she said.

"And I was there because . . . ?"

"Our grampa died. You came for the funeral."

"When's the funeral?"

"Today at two."

"And you came to get me because . . . ?"

"My mom asked me to get you. We're cousins."

"Where am I from?"

"Boston."

Jake couldn't help himself. He started laughing.

"What's so funny?" she asked.

"Nothing. I'm just glad to be alive, that's all."

"Of course you are. That was a bad fall. Let me go get Search and Rescue now."

"No, that's okay. I can make it by myself. If you'll just help me a little." He painfully made his way to a standing position. Now he realized that he really had been having hunger pains. He was also dying of thirst. *That's why I haven't been thinking very clearly,* he thought.

"Jake, look up there. It's way too steep. Let me go get some help."

45

By then the old Jake had returned. "I don't have time to wait around, okay? I've got to get to Seattle."

His tone surprised her. "You don't have to yell at me," she said.

Because he needed her help, he decided there was no reason to antagonize her. Antonio to the rescue. "How insensitive of me," he said softly. "What I meant to say is, please help me. We've got to at least try, don't we?"

That seemed to satisfy her. "All right, I'll help you."

He put his arm around her shoulder, and slowly they made their way over fallen trees, boulders, and prickly bushes. The physical exertion now made it very clear to Jake how hungry, thirsty, and weak he really was.

Halfway to the top, he had to stop to rest. He leaned on Andrea for support as they both tried to catch their breath. Their foreheads were covered with sweat, their arms draped around each other for support.

As he gazed into her beautiful, brown eyes, she gave him a friendly smile. He didn't take it personally because, by then, he knew she was the kind of person who smiles at everyone.

Because he was leaning so close to her for support, he could feel her stomach rising and falling as she also tried to catch her breath. At first he wasn't sure why that intrigued him so much, but then he realized it was because the actresses on *Wheels* avoided breathing normally for fear their stomachs would show. Andrea was much more natural. He liked that.

He felt light-headed and was afraid he was going to pass out. "I'd better sit down," he said, dropping onto a rock and lowering his head between his knees.

"You want me to get you some water?" she asked.

"Please," he said softly. She left. After that he either passed out or fell asleep.

The next thing he knew, Andrea was standing over him,

her hands cupped together to form a small reservoir. "I brought you some water," she said.

He sat up. She stood in front of him and, by slowly tipping her cupped hands, dribbled some water into his mouth.

"Where did you get this?" he asked.

"Down there."

He looked at a small stream at the bottom of the canyon, maybe a hundred yards of nearly impassable terrain from where they were. "You carried water up from there in your hands?" he asked.

She nodded. "It took me four tries. It kept leaking out."

He had always prided himself on being physically fit and emotionally distant. Now he was losing it in both areas. "I can't believe you'd do that for me," he said, his wavering voice barely above a whisper. Tears were gathering in his eyes. "I was so thirsty, and you gave me water. It was the best water I've ever had."

"A little salty, though, right?" she asked with a smile.

"No, not at all. But why go to all that work just for me?"

She patted him on the back. "Hey, c'mon, we're family, right? We've got to look out for each other."

He knew he should tell her the truth, but he didn't. He told himself it was because he still needed her help to get back to the cabin. But there was another reason. He'd never met anyone like her before, and he didn't want their time together to end any sooner than necessary. *I'll tell her, just not yet,* he thought.

"Right," he said. "Cousins got to stick together."

They started up the steep hillside again. She was stronger than she looked, and without her, he never would have made it.

He was surprised how weak he felt. "I'm sorry to be so much trouble," he said, the next time they stopped to catch their breath.

"Don't worry about it. You'd do the same for me."

He had to sit down again to rest. For a few minutes he sat there without saying anything, just trying to meet his body's demand for air. And then, finally, he could talk again. "How can you be so strong, so beautiful, and so good, all at the same time?"

With a silly grin on her face, she wagged her head. "Well, I can see you're easy to please."

"No, that's just it. I'm not. But I do recognize real beauty when I see it."

She put her hand on his forehead. "I was afraid of this— you're hallucinating," she teased.

"I'm serious. I will never forget how much trouble you went through to bring me water," he said, choking on the words.

"Glad to help out. Now let's see if we can make it the rest of the way."

Finally they made it up the hill to where the trail was. They stopped to rest before starting out again. They were quite a sight. The bottom of her dress was uneven and jagged where she'd ripped fabric to make a bandage for the cut on his leg. He had scratches and bruises all over him. And they were both perspiring.

"We made it, Jake," she said. "The rest is downhill from here."

"That's what I'm afraid of," he said quietly. He knew he'd miss her when he left town.

I should tell her the truth now, he thought.

"You want to sing a few songs?" she asked. "I'll start." She started to sing . . . "Happy trails to you, until we meet again." She sang it all the way through, and then asked him to join in. He couldn't do it. He was too embarrassed, but he liked hearing her sing.

I'll tell her. Just not yet.

"You want me to teach you songs from girls camp?" she asked. "It's a once-in-a-lifetime opportunity. Some friends and I taught a guy these songs once, but then we had to kill him. I'll share them with you, but only if you promise never to tell anyone."

"I promise."

They started down the trail.

"'If you're happy and you know it, clap your hands . . . ,'" she sang out, without embarrassment.

He couldn't walk fast, but he didn't have to lean on her like before. In a way, he missed that.

When they reached the cabin, Jake asked her to find something for him to eat. She located a box of Saltine crackers. He downed a couple of glasses of water, grabbed a packet of the crackers, and went into the bathroom to tend to his injuries. Andrea said she'd wait for him on the porch.

"Jake, you want me to run home, get a car and take you to the hospital?" she asked from a rocking chair on the porch.

He didn't want to go to the hospital because he'd have to show ID and then she'd know he wasn't her cousin. "No, it's okay, really. It's just a few scratches."

"I've been thinking. We should have a ceremony, so people can thank you for donating money to keep the pool open. We could get the mayor, and city council, and, of course, the kids who go swimming every day. We can do it tomorrow if you want."

He realized he must not let her give the cashier's check to the city. As delightful as she was, he was not going to waste fifteen thousand dollars to keep a swimming pool open.

I'll tell her the truth and get my money back, but just not yet, he thought.

"I'd rather keep it quiet, if that's okay with you," he called back.

"You'd rather the gift be anonymous?" she asked. "That

makes me respect you even more. Has anyone ever told you what a wonderful guy you are?"

Just me, he thought as he checked his abs in the mirror, something he'd been doing since he was a sophomore in high school.

He came out of the bathroom. Through the front screen door, he could see Andrea sitting in a rocking chair. Seeing her there made it seem like a scene from the Old West. Like if they were married and living on a small homestead, trying to survive the cold winters and short growing season. Maybe there was even a child on the way.

In slacks, but barefoot and not wearing a shirt, carrying his shoes and socks, he opened the screen door and walked onto the porch. He sat on the top step and began putting on his shoes and socks.

"Where's your shirt?" she asked.

Jake cleared his throat. "I thought you'd like to see me this way."

She looked confused. "What for?"

He felt a little foolish. "I guess I misunderstood you," he said.

"Don't get me wrong—you do look good without a shirt. You must have worked hard to get in this kind of shape. But for me, it's sort of like when someone makes you a fruitcake for Christmas. You know they went to a lot of trouble, but you're really not sure it was worth it." She started giggling, then caught herself. "That wasn't very nice, was it?"

"Don't worry about it." He went inside, put his shirt on, and came back out. "Sorry about that," he said when he returned.

"No harm done, but for a minute there, it was like being in ninth grade all over again."

"What happened in ninth grade?"

"Guys were going through these tremendous growth streaks. They used to strut around the halls, trying to look tough, or macho, or something. I could never figure out what they were trying to do, but, you know, that's the way it is in ninth grade." She started laughing. "Let's see, Jake, you're about ready to graduate from ninth grade, aren't you?"

"You said you liked to look at me."

"Okay, I confess, I said that. I just didn't think you'd let it go to your head, that's all. I mean, are you that—"

"Shallow?" he suggested, still smarting from the newspaper story about him in the Sunday *Tribune*.

"Hmm . . . shallow? Actually I was thinking immature, but . . . yeah, sure, shallow works."

"Anything else about me you'd care to trash?" he asked.

She looked worried. "I've gone too far, haven't I? You're getting mad at me now."

It was true. He was getting mad, but he didn't want her to know it. "No, not at all. I'm always looking for ways to improve."

"You sure?"

"Positive. What other constructive criticism do you have for me? I'm serious."

"Jake, I do like you. You know that, don't you?"

"Yeah, sure."

"Okay, good. I just don't want you getting mad at me."

"I promise I won't. It's like I said before. I want to learn as much as I can from you."

"That still amazes me. I guess I've been around too many jerks lately."

"What can I do that would make a girl like you be interested in me? I mean, if we weren't cousins."

Andrea hesitated saying anything.

"I'm serious."

"Well, okay, just one more thing and then I'll shut up. Let's talk about that shirt."

He liked the shirt because it showed off his build. "What about it?"

"Where'd you get it? The Humpty Dumpty Store for Little Kids?" She did a combination of laughing and apologizing at the same time. "Sorry, that wasn't fair. I'm really sorry. I shouldn't have said that." And then she lost it.

He started laughing too. "You big faker! You're not one bit sorry."

"No, really, I am."

He went inside and put on his light jacket over his shirt, then came out again.

"That's better," she said. "And I am sorry if I hurt your feelings, okay?"

"Hey, don't worry about it. We're cousins, right? So we can say things in the way of constructive criticism we'd never say to people outside the family."

"You're such a good sport, Jake."

"Thanks. But, really, what *do* you look for in a guy?"

She didn't answer for a few moments. Then she said, "The things I saw in you the first time we met—generosity, compassion, sensitivity."

"Thanks. Look, I'm sorry about coming out here with my shirt off. I guess I wasn't thinking very clearly." He touched the bruise on his forehead. "That fall must have jumbled some brain cells."

"I understand completely. You've been through a lot today."

"You have *no* idea," he said with a faint smile.

"And you don't mind me making suggestions?" she asked.

"No, not at all. I mean, we're cousins, so it's okay. I'm sure I can learn things from you that'll help me someday when I meet the girl of my dreams."

"Sure, I'd be glad to help that way."

They were looking into each other's eyes again. "Who knows? Maybe she'll be just like you," he said.

Andrea broke eye contact. "Except she won't be your cousin."

"No, she won't, that's for sure."

Jake was enjoying this game, but he did have business that needed to be taken care of. "Oh, I have a question about the cashier's check. When were you thinking of giving it to the city?"

"Well, since you don't want a ceremony, I guess I'll just go to the city office tomorrow and give it to Mr. Stephenson. He's in charge of the park and swimming pool."

"I'd like to go with you when you do that."

"Of course," she said. "When would you like to see him?"

"I don't know. Maybe tomorrow or the next day. It really doesn't matter. I'll tell you when I'm ready."

"Sure. I can hardly wait to see the expression on his face when we give it to him."

As much as Jake was enjoying getting to know Andrea, he knew he wouldn't rest until he had his check back. "Yeah, that'll be something, all right," he said.

Andrea looked at her watch. "Are you feeling well enough to go to the funeral?" she asked.

"Sure, no problem. I don't have the right clothes though."

"Grampa has some things in his closet. You could try one of his suits on."

The western-style suit hanging in Grampa's closet wasn't one Jake would have bought, but it was pretty close to his size. *Andrea's grampa must have been a pretty big man,* he thought. He selected an ugly tie with images of trout on it and was just finishing knotting it when a car pulled up.

"Andrea, where have you been? I expected you home hours ago."

Jake recognized a mother's tone of voice when he heard it. He stepped quickly to the sink and turned on the faucet so they'd think he was using the bathroom. Then he returned to the window so he could listen in on what they were saying.

"Jake and I climbed to the lookout. We both felt Grampa was there with us."

"Jake? Your cousin's name is Cameron."

"He goes by Jake now," Andrea said.

"Well, no matter. Your dad is already at the church. If we don't get going, we'll miss the viewing. I can't believe you were so late."

"We would've come sooner but Jake had an accident. He's okay, though. Just a few bruises and some scratches."

"I really could've used you at home."

"Sorry, Mom. Oh, you'll never believe what Jake did. He gave me a cashier's check for fifteen thousand dollars to keep the swimming pool running for the rest of the summer."

"What! Are you sure? People don't go around giving away that kind of money."

"Jake is a very caring person. He said that even though he'd planned on using the money to buy a Corvette, this was more important."

"Why would he do that?" her mom asked.

"He likes to help others. He's kind and generous . . . and . . ."

"And what?"

"Mom, I don't know if I should say this or not, but, my gosh, he looks like some kind of a movie star. It's not just his looks either. He asks me questions about the meaning of life. And he has so much respect for me. I've never met anyone like him before."

"Andrea! The boy is your cousin."

"I know that, okay?"

Jake came out of the cabin wearing Grampa's suit. "Well, hello. It's been a long time, hasn't it?" he said with his best Antonio smile.

54

A short time later they pulled away from the cabin. "How was your trip?" Andrea's mom asked.

"It was good."

"And how are your folks?"

"They're fine. Everyone's fine."

When they pulled into the driveway, Andrea said, "I'll go get ready," and dashed into the house.

"How is your mom's arthritis?" Andrea's mom asked.

Jake panicked. Without answering, he asked, "Would it be all right if I used your bathroom?"

While Jake went into the house, Andrea's mother stepped next door to speak to a neighbor.

A few moments later he heard water running in an upstairs bathroom. Then the phone began to ring. There was no one else to answer it, so, after five or six rings, he picked it up.

"Hello."

"Hello. This is Cameron. You're probably wondering what happened to me."

Jake tried to sound older. "Cameron? My gosh, we've been worried sick about you."

"Who is this?"

"Who do you think it is?" Jake asked.

"Uncle Albert?" Cameron guessed.

"Yes, that's right. Where are you?"

"I'm in a hospital in Detroit. I fell in the train and broke my leg."

"So you're not coming to the funeral? The family will be so disappointed."

"I'll come as soon as I can," Cameron said.

"Look, there's no need for you to come all the way out here after just getting out of the hospital."

"But I want to come," Cameron said.

"All I'm saying is, think about it. By the time you get

55

here, the funeral will be over, and most of the family will have gone."

"I suppose you're right."

"Cameron, let me ask you a question. How's your mom's arthritis?"

It was a long explanation. Jake took mental notes so he'd be able to pass them on to Andrea's mom.

"We have to go to the funeral now, Cameron. Thanks for calling, but do yourself a favor. Save your strength and don't bother coming out here."

He hung up and immediately turned his attention to finding the cashier's check. Andrea was still in the shower and her mom was outside talking to a neighbor, so Jake had the freedom to go wherever he wanted.

He found Andrea's bedroom on the second floor and began looking around for the cashier's check. Her room was intriguing. It was neatly organized and a wide sill under one of the dormer windows was piled with a collection of stuffed bears. The posters hanging on the wall weren't of rock groups or movie stars but, instead, something called "Mormonads."

He could hear Andrea singing in the shower. He quickly rummaged through her desk drawers looking for the check. No luck. There was a book lying open on top of the desk. A passage was marked in red. He read it.

And when ye shall receive these things, I would exhort you that ye would ask God, the Eternal Father, in the name of Christ, if these things are not true; and if ye shall ask with a sincere heart, with real intent, having faith in Christ, he will manifest the truth of it unto you, by the power of the Holy Ghost.

The book looked like some kind of bible, and Jake thumbed the pages. Nearly every page had parts that had been carefully marked in red. There were some loose papers stuffed into the book. He turned it upside down and shook. Several papers fell out, but no check.

The shower stopped. Jake didn't have much time. He stuffed the papers back in the book, then checked the center desk drawer once again. Still no luck.

When he heard the front door open, he quietly closed the drawer and left the room.

"Andrea, we really need to get going or we're going to be late," Andrea's mom called out.

Jake came down the stairs.

"What were you doing upstairs?" Andrea's mom asked.

"I just went up to tell Andrea to hurry."

"What did she say?"

"She said she would."

They heard the bathroom door open. "I'm almost ready."

"Please hurry!" Andrea's mom said.

Jake didn't want to have a long conversation with Andrea's mom because he was afraid she'd find out he was an impostor. "If you don't mind, I'd like to go in the garden and think about Grampa until Andrea is ready."

"Please do. Grampa was the one who did our garden."

Jake walked outside. *Big deal, it's a garden, so what?* he thought.

* * * * *

At the church, Jake was introduced to Andrea's father. He was wearing a western-style suit and bolo tie and was a stout man, nearly bald. He seemed as good-natured as Andrea.

"Dad, this is Cameron. He goes by Jake now though," she said quietly. The two men shook hands.

He clapped Jake on the shoulder in a friendly way, then said, "We're glad you could make it. You don't look the way I imagined you would, but, of course it's been a long time since you were here."

"That was a long time ago, Daddy. We were both only two years old. Mom was talking to me last night. She has a picture of the two of us, when we were toddlers, in the bathtub together. She said we were both real cute back then," Andrea said, smiling.

"We still are," Jake said.

Andrea giggled. "Just ask us, right?"

"I'm glad you two cousins are getting along so well," her dad said. "But we need to get to the viewing."

The extended family was gathered in a carpeted room where the body lay in an open casket. The room was filled with bouquets of flowers and with people. To Jake, it looked like the setting for some kind of wake, but he was surprised at the noise. People were conversing quite loudly, and some of them even laughed as they paid their respects and visited with Andrea and her parents and the other mourners. Jake stood to the side, observing what for him was a strange ritual. He wasn't caught up emotionally in the proceedings and enjoyed watching Andrea as she greeted the people who filed in a steady stream into the room.

She really is different from any other girl I've ever known, Jake thought. He loved watching her face. She looked sad, but brightened each time she greeted another person. She hugged almost everyone who filed by, and sometimes smiled and cried at the same time. She seemed to be comfortable in that setting, even with the open casket right next to her. Being in the same room with a dead body seemed weird to Jake.

Finally, an officiator dressed in a dark suit called for everyone's attention. He said it was time for "family prayer" and called on one of Andrea's uncles to pray, which he did in an emotional voice. At first Jake was critical because the prayer didn't seem very professional. He looked around the room. Everyone's eyes were closed. If nothing else, they seemed sincere.

At the end of the prayer, everyone said amen. Jake also thought that was a little strange. He thought that one "amen" from the minister or priest would have done the trick.

Then it was time to close the casket, but before he did so, the mortician invited the family members to pay their final respects.

Andrea took Jake's hand and they approached the coffin together. She wept as she looked at Grampa for the last time. Sniffling, she said, "He looks good, doesn't he?"

Jake studied the body in the coffin. Andrea's grandfather *had* been a big man, barrel-chested and broad shouldered. His full head of gray hair was combed back in a pompadour style and, with a slight smile on his lips, he looked as though he might be sleeping. "Yes," Jake said, "he looks very peaceful."

"I keep expecting him to get up," Andrea said. "I wish I could be around when the Millennium begins."

Jake thought she was talking about the year 2000. "You will be," he said.

"You're right," she said, squeezing his hand as though he'd said something very comforting.

Jake let loose of Andrea's hand and put his arm around her shoulder and drew her close. *That's what Cameron would do,* he thought.

"I'm glad you came," she said, leaning into him.

"Why?"

"You've been a strength to me. The only time I saw you almost lose it was when I first met you at the train station."

He nodded. "I don't think I'll ever forget the way I felt," he said truthfully.

With the casket closed, the family was escorted into the chapel for the funeral. Andrea sat close to Jake and held his hand for comfort. Jake didn't mind.

As Andrea sang "Amazing Grace," Jake thought she was the most beautiful girl he'd ever seen. Almost like a real angel, and when she returned to sit next to Jake, he reached for her hand. "Good job," he whispered.

"Thanks." She squeezed his hand.

A friend of the family was the first to speak: "I've known Boyd Reece for at least thirty years. He was the kind of man you hope your children will someday become . . . a man of faith, integrity, and compassion."

Jake looked sideways at Andrea. Her eyes were damp, but she was also smiling as she listened. Jake had only been to one funeral before. His mother's sister had died when Jake was just a boy. He remembered the service being very dark, with everyone wearing black and candles burning. The services for Andrea's grandfather weren't sad at all. Those who spoke remembered his good qualities, and the man Andrea called the bishop talked about how everyone would eventually be resurrected and reunited in heaven. That was news to Jake.

After the service, they rode to the cemetery where Andrea's dad said a prayer over the gravesite, and then everyone went back to the church for a luncheon.

* * * * *

During the luncheon, Jake slipped out and walked to the train station. There, among the weeds, he found his cell phone.

He called Christopher who began the conversation with, "Are you in Seattle yet?"

"Well, actually, no, I'm in Montana. I had an accident that kind of held me up."

"What kind of accident?"

"I ran into something in the middle of the night and knocked myself out."

Christopher wasn't much for expressions of sympathy. "Can you walk?"

"Yeah."

"Good. When are you leaving for Seattle?"

"I'll go tomorrow morning. Make an appointment with Dwight Stone for tomorrow night."

"Done."

"Oh, one other thing, I met a girl. Her name is Andrea. She's different than any other girl I've ever known."

"Let her be different after you make a deal with Stone. That's what counts. After that, I don't care what you do."

* * * * *

Jake returned to the church and helped put up chairs and tables, then went home with Andrea.

At six-thirty, Jake and Andrea were sitting in the living room together, leafing through a family album. He saw her grow up with each new page.

"Can I ask a big favor?" she said.

"I guess so."

"Grampa had this old fishing hat. He wore it every time we hiked into Harrison Lake to go fishing. I found a note in the hat last night. Grampa asked me to go back and leave his fishing hat there. I've cut it into tiny pieces, and I want to climb a rock face and scatter the pieces to the wind. I talked Dad into going there with me tomorrow. Would you come with us? It'd mean so much to me. We'll camp over that night and then come out the next day."

"I'm sorry. I can't. I need to leave for Seattle tomorrow."

"I see," she said softly.

"Sorry."

"No, that's fine," she said, then stood up. "Excuse me." She hurried out of the house.

Jake felt bad about turning her down. A minute later he went after her to try to explain it.

He found her at the cabin, sitting in one of the rocking

61

chairs on the porch. The sun had dropped behind the mountains, and it was getting cool. Andrea had a shawl around her shoulders.

"Mind if I join you?" he asked.

She nodded.

He sat in the other rocking chair. "My best friend is depending on me to go to Seattle. His future is at stake. Mine too. It's very important."

She nodded, looked away, and wouldn't talk to him.

"Are you mad at me?" he asked gently.

She shook her head no.

"It's okay to say how you feel. I do it all the time."

She looked miserable. "I don't."

"I'll be you, and you be me, okay?" He gently took the shawl from her and put it on his head, like a scarf. He stood up, pointed his finger at her, and in a high falsetto, cried out, "Jake, are you in this family, or aren't you?"

"I've got to go to Seattle tomorrow," she said in her imitation of a man's voice.

Jake put his hands on his hips like his mother always did when she was mad.

"If you asked me to stay, I'd drop everything else and do it! I need somebody I can count on! Like I could count on Grampa!"

Through her tears, Andrea smiled, and, playing the role of Jake, she stood up and pretended she was about to lift her shirt up. "You want to see my abs?"

They both burst out laughing. It was then he saw both dimples. It was worth the wait. He wrapped the shawl around her neck and drew her to him.

"Oh, my gosh!" she said. "That was so funny."

"You got me that time, didn't you?" he teased.

"I guess I did."

He was going to make some funny remark, but when he looked at her, their eyes met, and their smiles faded.

"Cousin Jake," she said softly.

It felt so peaceful being there with her. He gently laid the shawl around her shoulders and kissed her on the forehead. "If you really want me to go with you and your dad tomorrow, of course I will."

* * * * *

That night, after walking Andrea home, Jake returned to Grampa's cabin.

He dreaded calling Christopher. Whenever he got mad, Christopher's voice became thin and high. Like now. "Dwight Stone has two Emmy Awards, you know! Calling him is not exactly like ordering from Domino's."

"This is the last delay. I promise."

"Two days you say? Where are you again?"

"West Glacier, Montana."

"All right. I'll meet you at the train station Friday morning in West Glacier, on the same train you originally scheduled. And then we'll both go see Dwight Stone."

* * * * *

Dwight Stone, forty-two years old, fast becoming a legend in the film and television industries, ran his personal identification card through the scanner at the security gate, then proceeded along the narrow road leading to his mansion overlooking Puget Sound. His cell phone rang, and he picked it up. "Yeah?."

"Mr. Stone, this is Christopher Bergstrom. I'm the director of *Wheels*. I talked to your secretary yesterday."

"I was supposed to see Jake Petricelli today. What happened?" Stone demanded.

"Well, actually, there's been a death . . . in the family."

Stone pulled into his driveway. His wife's car was parked

there. The backseat and open trunk were full of suitcases and boxes and clothes.

Christopher continued. "Because of the funeral, Jake and I were wondering if we could reschedule."

Stone jumped out of his car, still carrying the cell phone in his hand. "Vera! Don't do this to me!" he shouted.

Vera Stone breezed past Dwight. Carrying an armload of dresses, she threw them on the front seat of the car and turned to go back into the house.

"Vera, look, okay, I know you're upset with me, and I have it coming, I'll go to counseling with you, like you asked. Just don't leave me!"

Stone followed her as she went in for another load. "I told you last time that it was the last time, and I meant it. Good-bye, Dwight!"

Vera sorted through a stack of CD's, picked out the ones she wanted, and headed back to her car in the driveway. She got in the car, started it, and slammed her door closed.

Dwight Stone stood next to the car, his arms extended, and shouted, "Vera! Don't do this! We can work something out!"

Vera lurched into reverse and backed the car out of the driveway.

"Vera!"

She squealed her tires and drove away.

Christopher continued, "Look, if this isn't a good time to talk, I can call you back."

Dwight Stone watched Vera speed away. Then he looked down at the cell phone and, in a fit of rage, threw it over a cliff into the sea.

5

"He'll never make it," Andrea's dad said as he and Andrea watched Jake, his backpack crammed to overflowing, lose his balance and nearly fall as he forded the Middle Fork of the Flathead River.

As Andrea and her dad had done a few minutes before, Jake walked barefoot across the slippery rocks lining the bottom of the shallow river. His boots and socks were slung over his backpack to keep them dry. The water was numbingly cold and the current swift.

Andrea and her dad were waiting across the river at the trailhead for Harrison Lake, where a sign declared an ominous warning: *Beware! You Are Entering Bear Country.*

"If his feet go out from under him," her dad said, "he'll be washed a mile downstream before we can do anything about it. That's if he's lucky. Of course, his backpack could sink him to the bottom, then we'd never even find the body."

Jake eventually made it across the river. He struggled up a short hill to where Andrea and her father were waiting. He was so out of breath he was panting like a dog. "Are we there yet?"

"No, this is just the trailhead," Andrea said.

"Trailhead?" he gasped. "What does that mean?"

"It means the beginning of the trail," Andrea said.

Jake panicked. "Are you saying that what we've done so far doesn't even count?"

"Afraid not," she answered, watching him stagger under the weight of his pack. "My gosh, Jake, what've you got in that backpack of yours anyway?"

"Just the basics." Jake had insisted on making a private trip to the general store before they left town.

"Let me see," Andrea said.

Jake took off his backpack and sat down to dry his feet and put on his shoes and socks. He and Andrea were wearing identical wool shirts and baseball caps. Jake had bought them when he went shopping.

Andrea pulled a heavy cast-iron frying pan from his backpack. "What's this for?" she asked.

"We'll need something to cook the bacon in."

"You brought bacon?" Andrea asked. She rummaged through the backpack and came up with a two-pound package of bacon.

"You can't take bacon into a wilderness area," her dad said.

"I like bacon."

"Just last summer," her dad said, "a hiker was killed by a bear. The man stored bacon in his tent when he went to bed. The bear came for the bacon and ended up killing him."

Andrea pulled out a miniature, battery-operated TV. "You can't take this either."

"Let me guess," Jake said. "Last summer the same bear and a hiker couldn't agree on what channel to watch. Right?"

Andrea suppressed a grin. Then she pulled a canister of Turbo Muscle Power from the backpack. "What on earth is this?"

Jake blushed. "It's just something I take."

"Well, I think you can get along without it for a day or two, don't you?"

"It gives me energy," Jake said, still gasping for breath.

"Food'll do that too. You might try it sometime," she said.

She removed her backpack, quickly took off her boots and socks, got the car keys from her dad, and then forded the river in about one-fourth the time it had taken Jake. She gave the bacon to a family packing their van to leave, and after she had stowed the frying pan, the TV, and the Turbo Muscle Power in the trunk of the car, she started back across the river.

"How can she do all that when I'm still trying to catch my breath?" Jake asked her dad.

"It's the elevation," her dad explained. "There's not as much oxygen at higher elevations. We're used to it, but you're not."

Andrea returned, then sat down to dry off her feet and put on her socks and boots. "It's getting late. We need to get going."

A minute later they were on the trail. Jake was privately relieved how much lighter his backpack felt. "If we don't have bacon, what are we going to have for breakfast?" he asked as they began hiking.

"Oatmeal," she said.

"You're kidding! You're going to eat oatmeal without a mom around? What's wrong with you people?"

* * * * *

Andrea and her dad hiked along at a comfortable pace, followed at a distance by Jake, who couldn't seem to keep up no matter how slow they went.

Five hours later they came over a rise and saw Harrison Lake. Andrea called back to Jake, who was far behind them on the trail. "Just a little bit more, Jake! C'mon, you can make it!"

"It'll be a while before he catches up," her dad said. "I'll go set up camp."

Pointing up to a ledge on a cliff, Andrea said, "Jake and I will scatter the pieces of Grampa's fishing hat from up there."

Her dad looked at a rock face that rose above them. "You think you can get him up there?"

"I'll teach him how to climb. Like Grampa taught me. So, in a way, it's like I'm passing it on from Grampa to Jake."

* * * * *

An hour later Jake was desperately clinging to a cliff and fearing for his life. From fifteen feet above him, Andrea belayed him with a climbing rope.

"That's it, Jake. Now swing across with one leg over to that ledge and then support yourself with that handhold."

"What handhold? All I see is a tiny bump the size of a strawberry."

"That's a very good handhold."

"Now I know why you have no friends. They've all died climbing, right?"

"Just the wimps, Jake, just the wimps."

"I'll get you for that, Andrea, just you wait."

"Hey, buddy, anytime. Come and get me. I'm right up here."

He sighed. "I know. That's the problem."

"Look, I'll have absolutely no respect for you unless you make it up here."

"Okay, here I come." Jake made the move sideways to the handhold. Below him was a sheer thirty-foot drop.

"Good job! The rest is easy. Now just cram your hand into that crack and pull yourself up. Whatever you do, don't look down."

He looked down and froze. "Too late. I already have."

"Let's talk about something else then." They heard the laughing call of a loon. "You hear that? It's a loon," she said.

"It'll probably be the last sound I'll hear."

"The sound of a loon reminds me of a poem I once read," she said.

"I hate poems," he grumbled.

"I've written a few poems," she said.

"What I mean is, I hate *some* poems," he said.

"Really? What's your favorite poem?" she asked.

Jake got a little courage and continued his ascent. "It's about this guy who stops in the woods during a snowstorm."

"Oh, you mean 'Stopping by Woods on a Snowy Evening'?"

"That's what it's about, all right."

"No, that's the title. It's by Robert Frost."

Jake was now less than five feet from Andrea. "He didn't get too creative with the title, did he?" A short time later he pulled himself onto the ledge where Andrea was. From that vantage point they could see most of Harrison Lake. It was long and narrow, and its water was a dark blue-green.

She tousled his hair. "You made it. Good job."

"Say to me, 'Youda man!'" he said.

"Do I have to?"

"C'mon, Andrea. I just risked my life for you. It's the least you can do."

She gave him a pained expression. "All right, if you insist. You are the man," she said in a dull monotone.

"What's the matter with you, Girl? You got no soul?"

"There's no pleasing you, is there?"

"Look, it's one word, okay? *Youda*. And you have to do this with your hands." He showed her a move he'd learned from a rap group. "Okay, try it again."

She gave him an exaggerated sigh. "The things I put up with. Okay, let me try it. Youda man!"

"That was better. This time, say it like you really mean it."

"I'm not going to keep saying it, okay? My gosh, Jake, are you always this insecure?"

"Yeah, pretty much."

There wasn't much room on the ledge so they ended up sitting much closer than cousins normally would. He put his arm around her to conserve space. "Hmm . . . maybe this was worth it, after all," he whispered in her ear.

She didn't take him seriously. "Yeah, sure, Cousin."

"So, did I pass your test of manhood?" he asked.

"Excuse me? Test of manhood? It was a woman who had to drag you up here."

"That is so unfair. True, of course, but still . . . "

She tried imitating Arnold Schwarzenegger. "I owe all my strength to Turbo Muscle Power."

He made a half-hearted attempt to poke her in the ribs with his elbow. "You are so predictable! I knew you couldn't let that go."

"Sorry," she said, trying to be serious. But it was too much to hope for. "Turbo Boy to the rescue!" That broke her up.

"Go ahead, laugh, make fun of me, have a good time at my expense."

"Okay, thanks," she said, laughing even harder.

"Actually, that was supposed to make you feel guilty."

"I wonder why it didn't," she teased.

"Because you're a cold, heartless wrench."

"Excuse me? *Wrench?* Did you say *wrench?*" She burst out laughing. "It's not *wrench.* It's *wench.*"

He shrugged. "Whatever."

She rested her hand on the sleeve of his shirt. "I hope you don't get tired of me teasing you all the time."

"No, not at all."

"Grampa would enjoy seeing us together. He was so

much fun to be with. I'm sorry you didn't know him better. You'd have liked him, Jake."

"From what you've said, I'm sure I would have."

She sighed. "Well, I guess we'd better do what we came up here for."

She retrieved the plastic bag containing pieces of the old fishing hat, then stood up. She rested one hand on Jake's shoulder for support.

"Grampa, we're here, just like you asked. Cameron's here too. Except he goes by Jake now." She paused. "You were my *grampa,* but you were also my best friend. I could always talk to you about just about anything. The only one I've got like that now is Jake."

She opened the bag and tossed some of the fragments of the hat into the air, then turned to Jake. "That was west. You do north and east, and I'll finish up with south."

"I probably shouldn't do this."

"You're part of the family too. Please, Jake."

Jake stood up, took the bag and tossed a few of the pieces of cloth in two directions, then he gave the bag back to Andrea, who took what was left and tossed it.

"Sing the song you sang at the funeral," Jake suggested.

She sang "Amazing Grace," then sat down next to him. Together, they watched the clouds drift by and gazed at the mountains and the lake.

He rested his arm across her shoulder. Because it was just a friendly gesture, Andrea didn't seem to mind. They were wearing matching shirts, and when he glanced at her, he noticed that the fabric of his sleeve blended with the cloth in her shirt. It was a momentary illusion, but for a second, he couldn't tell where his arm ended and her shoulder began. It was a nice feeling—to be connected in that way with her.

She talked about Grampa, and Jake tried to be a good

71

listener, but it was a new experience for him. He'd never been someone who people came to with their problems.

All I have to do is try to do what Andrea would do if somebody came to her with a problem. His male ego fought against the idea. He found himself having a debate with himself. *You're trying to be like a girl? What is wrong with you anyway?*

It won't kill me to try to be a little more understanding.

Next thing you know you'll be playing with dolls.

Look, her grandfather just died. She needs somebody to talk to.

Why are you wasting time with her anyway? She's not that good-looking.

I don't agree. She's beautiful. But even if she weren't, are you saying I should only be nice to girls who meet a certain minimum standard of beauty?

That's exactly what I'm saying.

You're wrong. Not only that, but what if Christopher's grandfather died? Wouldn't it be good if he could talk to me about it?

Who made you Mr. Sensitivity all of a sudden?

You know the answer to that question. I've learned a lot from Andrea.

Oh, man, I can't stand this, his male ego complained.

As the sun was about to set, he tuned in to what Andrea was saying. "Thanks for letting me ramble on about Grampa," she said.

"Anytime. It helped me feel closer to him too."

"We'd better start down. Thanks for everything, Jake. You've been a big help today."

Jake felt guilty. "Some day you may resent me for being a part of this. Just remember that when we were up here, I really did want to be a help to you."

"Of course. I know that."

There was nothing more he could say. If he told her the

truth, she might not want him around anymore. *I'll tell her everything. Just not yet.*

She began to prepare the rope for their descent. "Have you ever done any rappelling?"

"No, but I've watched it on TV. Does that count?"

Andrea carefully rigged him up for rappelling. "Okay, what you need to do is keep one hand on the rope and lean back, away from the cliff." She showed him how to play out some rope, then said, "Go ahead."

Jake stood there trying to get up enough courage to do what she asked. "I guess this is a case where I need to trust you," he said.

"Just like I trust you."

Jake felt a twinge of conscience. He leaned back until he was almost perpendicular to the rock face.

"Now just jump out and let out some rope."

Jake tried it and was surprised when he didn't fall to his death. He quickly got the hang of it, and by the time he was near the bottom, he was no longer afraid.

"I did it!" he yelled up to her once he was down.

"Good job! Here I come."

Andrea came down quickly. Jake threw his arms around her. "If you'd been my Scoutmaster, I'd have made Eagle rank for sure."

"You'd have to be thrifty, brave, clean, and reverent though. You think you could manage that?"

"No, but two out of four isn't bad, right?"

"The question is, which two?"

"Good question." He brushed some stray strands of her hair away from her face and gazed into her eyes. "You know what? I love . . . " The words hung in the air. He wanted to say *I love you,* but he knew that would be a huge mistake. So he added, " . . . the great outdoors."

They might have kissed, but at the last minute, she shook her head and moved away. "This is so weird. I don't know what's going on here. You're a real charmer, Jake, and that's a fact. But don't waste it on a cousin, okay? Let's take care of the rope, then go find my dad."

* * * * *

Supper consisted of a packet of dried soup cooked up in hot water, followed by hot chocolate.

"You get enough, Jake?" her dad asked.

"Oh, yeah. I've had about as much as I can stand."

They did have an excellent dessert though. Toasted marshmallows, layered between graham crackers and chocolate. It wasn't just a dessert— it was a craft project because it took so much time to put together.

After dinner, they sat around the fire, gazing into the coals and listening to Andrea's dad tell stories about former trips to the area. While he talked, he rigged up some fishing gear. They could hear the call of the loon from the lake.

At ten-thirty, Andrea said she was going to get ready for bed. She went into the tent, leaving Jake and her dad together.

"What do you want me to call you?" Jake asked.

"Vernon is my name."

"But you go by Vern, right?"

"No, I go by Vernon."

"Is it okay if I call you Vernon?"

"Sure, that'd be fine. By the way, I'm going fishing in the morning," Vernon said. "I'll probably leave around five and return about eleven in the morning."

"Well, good luck, I hope you catch a lot of fish."

"I brought along an extra pole so you can fish too."

"No, that's okay," Jake said. "I'll probably just sleep in."

"I'd really like you to come with me," Vernon said.

"Well, since you put it that way, okay."

74

"You'll get to see the sun come up," Vernon said enthusiastically.

"Wow, lucky me," Jake said, resigned to his fate.

Vernon stood up and stretched. "Well, I guess it's about that time." He crawled into the tent.

Jake sat next to the fire, watching it turn to embers and finishing off the rest of the chocolate. He'd never seen the stars so bright or been anywhere where the air didn't have a tinge of diesel fuel smell to it.

He took in the smell of the smoke from the fire, then touched his nose to the sleeve of his new shirt and sampled that smell. He liked the shirt. It was large and gave him unlimited movement, and the natural fabric was somehow comforting to his skin.

Occasionally the laughing call of a loon came from the lake. Jake imagined that the loons were having a party, and, once in a while, one of them would burst out laughing at some joke. It made the darkness of the night seem less threatening.

At eleven, Jake decided to turn in. Andrea was against the wall of the tent, and Vernon was bedded down in the middle, in a position that left no doubt where Jake was to sleep.

Andrea didn't say anything when he entered the tent, and he wasn't sure if she was asleep or just didn't want to talk to him.

He got into his sleeping bag then wriggled out of his jeans. It was cold at first but eventually he warmed up.

After a time, Vernon began to snore. But this was no ordinary snore.

He would snort a couple of times and then there would be no sound, almost as if his body had forgotten how to breathe. The tension was unbearable. Jake wanted to shake him and say, "Take a breath, will you?" And then, just when it seemed he couldn't go another moment without breathing,

Vernon would make a sharp sucking sound as the air hissed into his body.

A few seconds later the whole process would be repeated.

"Jake, are you asleep?" Andrea whispered.

"No, but do me a favor and knock me out. That's the only way I'll get any sleep tonight."

She started giggling. "You want to go out by the fire and talk?" she asked.

Still in their sleeping bags, like a couple of giant caterpillars in their cocoons, they wriggled out of the tent. Jake put some wood on the fire. Andrea settled herself against a log next to the fire and pulled the sleeping bag up to her chin.

"Are you worried the bears will come and get us tonight?" she asked.

"If a bear comes by, it'll only be to complain about your dad's snoring."

"You're right. They're probably all holed up in some cave as far away from here as they can get," she added.

"Think they'd have any room for us?" he joked, wriggling over to sit next to her.

"Could be." She rested her head on his shoulder. "I love coming here. It always makes me happy. What do you do when you want to be happy?"

"I watch infomercials on TV. You never see any unhappy people on an infomercial. They've all lost weight, they've all trimmed and toned, they've all caught fish, or they've all made huge amounts of money in real estate. Take my word for it. There's nothing like a good infomercial for producing happiness."

"You are the strangest person I've ever met. It's hard to believe we're cousins."

"Tell me about it."

She gently poked him in the side. "So—you're going fishing with my dad in the morning, right?"

"Fishing is my life," he said dully.

"It will be if you spend much time with dad. He'll enjoy having you with him."

"That's my mission in life, to bring happiness to every member of your family, including you."

"Is that right?"

"Absolutely."

They were gazing into each other's eyes. "I didn't know that," she said softly.

It seemed almost inevitable when Jake kissed her. When they broke away, Andrea, with a silly grin on her face, whispered, "Daddy, Jake just kissed me. If that's not okay with you, tell me, because if I don't hear from you, we might do it again."

They waited. The only reply was just another couple of those raspy snores.

She smiled at him. "I guess it's okay then."

Their second kiss was much longer.

Suddenly she pulled away. "Well, that was . . . uhh . . . " She sounded flustered.

"Spectacular?" he suggested.

"Well, yeah, but, also, a little scary." She got up from the ground and, holding her sleeping bag around her, hopped to a log across the fire from him, then sat down.

They sat without saying anything for a few moments, then Andrea said, "Jake, the fact is we're cousins. I think we both need to start keeping that in mind."

"You know I was adopted though, right?" he asked.

"C'mon, be serious. I think we need to be very careful here."

"What if we weren't cousins?" he asked, trying to decide if he should tell her the truth or not.

"If we weren't cousins, then you wouldn't be here."

He let out a big sigh. "Good point."

"You want to try to get some sleep now?" she asked.

He shook his head. "Between listening to your dad snore and wanting to be snuggled next to you, I'd never get any sleep."

"What are you going to do then?" she asked.

Still wrapped in his sleeping bag, he stood up and maneuvered his way over to the tent. He reached in, grabbed his clothes and boots, and then hopped like a bunny away from the campfire into the darkness. "I'll sleep under the stars. See you in the morning."

"Poor Jake," she called out.

After he left, she said softly, "Poor me."

6

The sky was still black when Vernon found where Jake was sleeping. "Jake, wake up. It's time to go fishing."

Jake groaned. "It's still night."

"This is a good time for fishing. Besides, I have a flashlight."

Jake sat up and rubbed his eyes. "Do the fish have flashlights too?"

By the time they arrived at their destination, it was light enough to see shapes without a flashlight. Jake zipped up his light jacket, sat down on a log, and tried to stay warm. They were on a gravel beach near the inlet to the lake.

Vernon finished rigging up both fishing poles. "Have you ever done this before?" he asked.

"No, never have."

He showed Jake how to cast. They were using a clear plastic bubble, behind which they dragged a spinner, which was supposed to look like a swimming minnow. Jake doubted that it would work.

Vernon watched Jake cast a few times and then, satisfied his nephew could do it, he moved a ways off and started fishing.

Jake expected nothing. But, a few minutes later, as he reeled in, he felt a sudden strong tug on his line. At first he thought he'd hung up on a rock, but then a fish jumped out of the water. "I got one!" he shouted.

Vernon reeled in and came over to give advice. "Keep your pole up. That's it. Reel in steady. Okay, now what you want to do is, when you get the fish to the bank, don't try to lift it out of the water. Just drag it up on the bank and then I'll get hold of it and remove the hook."

Jake dragged the cutthroat trout onto the shore. Vernon knelt down and picked it up by the gills and showed it off. "It's a nice sized fish, Jake! Good job. We need to either release it or keep it. What's your choice?"

Suddenly Jake felt like "Mighty Fisherman." He wanted Andrea to see what he'd done. "I'm taking it back to camp. We'll have it for breakfast."

Vernon nodded his head, took a pair of pliers from his pocket, hit the fish in the head with the pliers, and put it in his creel.

They separated and started fishing again.

Jake ended up catching and releasing five other fish. In time he figured out what the spinner was doing. Several times he saw a fish following the shiny lure nearly up to the shore before breaking off the chase.

The two men stood there, close enough to talk, but too far away for any conversation that wasn't absolutely necessary.

Jake had never seen a sunrise, but he saw one that morning as the sun made its way over a nearby mountain, spreading its warmth and filling the world with promise. He felt as if every part of him was absorbing the beauty of that one glorious morning.

As he watched the sun fill the valley with light, he thought, *What else could I possibly be doing that would be better than this?*

After a couple of more hours of fishing though, Jake had had enough. He went over and sat on a boulder to keep Vernon company.

"You want to go back to camp?" Vernon asked.

"No, that's okay. I just thought I'd take a break, that's all. Keep fishing."

"Nice morning, huh?" Vernon asked.

Jake glanced at the beauty all around him. "I've never seen anything like this before."

Vernon nodded. "It grows on you. I've been coming here for years, and I never get tired of it."

"I can see why. I definitely want to come back here again someday."

"And fishing? You like that too?" Vernon asked.

"Yeah, I do. Thanks for teaching me."

"I'm just glad to have someone to go with."

On the next cast Vernon caught the biggest fish of the day. When he got it to shore, he carefully removed the hook from the fish's mouth and then gently released it back into the water.

"I would've kept it," Jake said.

"If I did that, it wouldn't be here when I come back the next time."

"True."

Jake removed his jacket and felt the warmth of the sun on his skin. Vernon didn't talk much. Jake was glad about that in a way. That meant Andrea's dad hadn't gotten him away just so he could lecture him about something.

"You think Andrea is up yet?" Vernon asked.

"I don't know. She ought to be."

"Yeah, she ought to be, but that doesn't mean she is. She likes to sleep in. Always has. Probably always will."

"Nothing wrong with that," Jake said.

"Nope, sure isn't. Lots of people do, that's for sure. You like to get up early?"

"I'm pretty much a sleeper-inner."

Vernon nodded. "Must be hereditary."

"I guess so."

81

"You and Andrea seem to be getting along real good," Vernon said.

Remembering last night's kiss, Jake felt a little guilty. That surprised him. Andrea certainly wasn't the first girl he'd ever kissed. Maybe it was pretending to be cousins that bothered him. But all he said was, "Yeah, we are. She's a lot of fun to be with."

"Having you here these last couple of days has been a big help to her. She was really close to Grampa."

"Yeah, I know. She's told me a lot about him."

"She's going to miss you when you go," Vernon said.

"I'll miss her too."

"You think you'll ever come back to Montana?"

"If you'll take me fishing again. I'd love to come back here someday."

Vernon smiled. "It's a deal. Anytime you want." He reeled in. "Well, I think the fish have quit biting. Let's go back to camp."

When they made it to the campsite, there was a small fire going. Andrea was in the tent. When she heard them coming, she did an imitation of a growling bear. "Rrrugh!"

"Oh no! There's a bear in the tent!" Jake cried out. "I just hope Andrea isn't in there too."

"Help me," Andrea cried out barely loud enough to be heard. She followed that up with another mean-spirited growl from the bear.

"She *is* in there with the bear!" Jake shouted. "We'd better go save her!"

"Sure, but how about if we have breakfast first?" Vernon said calmly. "I am *so* hungry. All I can think about now is eating."

The bear in the tent seemed surprised. "Rrrruuuh?"

"Good idea," Jake said. "We'll eat first and then worry about Andrea. You know, it's too bad I don't have my Turbo

Muscle Power with me. That could make a big difference if I have to fight the bear. Oh, well, too late now."

Andrea burst out of the tent. She'd pulled her hair back into a single braid.

"She's okay!" Jake cried out.

"No thanks to you two! I can't believe you were going to eat breakfast before rescuing me."

"Rescue *you?* Are you kidding?" her dad teased. "It was the bear I was worried about."

She tugged his fishing hat down over his eyes. "Well, maybe you should be a little worried about yourself."

Next she focused her pretended rage on Jake. "Hey, you, Turbo Boy!"

"You talking to me?"

She came behind him and knocked his hat off. "How could you be so mean to your favorite cousin?" She stood behind him with both hands on his shoulders.

"Favorite cousin? Hmmmm, let's see, who would that be?"

She leaned forward and to the side so that her face was very close to his.

"That would be me," she whispered.

"Oh, sure. You're right. I should have run into the tent and rescued you. What was I thinking?" That's what he said for the benefit of Vernon. What he said with his eyes was, *Do you have any idea how beautiful you are?*

Their silly smiles vanished as they gazed at each other. After a moment, she left to sit by her dad. "So, the mighty fishermen have returned. How'd you guys do?"

Vernon pulled a fish from his creel. "Look at what Jake caught."

"Jake, I can't believe it! You caught that?"

"Yeah, but your dad showed me what to do."

"He's the one who caught it though," her dad said. "We thought we'd have it for breakfast."

"That's great—as long as you don't expect me to cook it," Andrea said.

"That's your place in life," Jake teased, doing a bad imitation of Mountain Man. "We hunt and fish. You stay in camp, keep the fires burning, do all the cooking."

"Yeah, right," she scoffed.

Jake shrugged his shoulders in a gesture of defeat. "It was worth a shot," he said to Vernon.

Vernon nodded. "I could've told you it wouldn't work. Andrea pretty much does things her own way."

"What did you do while we were gone?" Jake asked.

"Oh, were you two gone? I didn't even notice."

"I don't believe that," Jake said. "You missed us."

"Why do you think that?"

"Because we're such good company," Jake answered.

"He's right there," Vernon said with a smile.

"For your information, I slept as long as I possibly could, got up, made a fire, did my hair, and wondered when you guys'd be back to fix me breakfast. If you hadn't shown up in the next ten minutes, I was going to take matters into my own hands, and cook my own."

"You were actually going to cook? You must've really been desperate," Vernon teased.

When they sat down to eat, Jake watched with disgust as Andrea and Vernon stirred dry packets of oatmeal into cups of hot water.

"You sure you don't want some?" Andrea asked.

"No thanks."

Andrea opened a packet, found a brown sugar lump and put it in Jake's mouth. It tasted good. Before long, he was eating some oatmeal with the brown sugar. "What a good boy you are to eat your oatmeal," she said, sounding like a mother.

Vernon cooked the trout for them. It was the best-tasting

fish Jake had ever had. He didn't even mind having to pick out the tiny bones.

After breakfast, Vernon decided to go fishing again.

Jake and Andrea found a field of flowers even more beautiful than the one near town by Grampa's cabin.

Andrea waved to her dad down by the lake to let him know where they were, and then she and Jake plopped down on the ground on their backs, their arms outstretched, fingers barely touching and watched puffy clouds drift over.

After a few minutes, Andrea fell asleep. Jake turned on his side and propped his head up with his hand and elbow so he could look at her as she slept. Her face was framed by a sea of delicate yellow and purple mountain flowers.

He took a blade of grass and lightly brushed the skin between her lip and nose. She wiggled her nose but didn't smile. That's how he knew she was really asleep.

I can't believe I'm just sitting around watching you snooze. You see what happens with no TV? But it's okay. I'm not complaining, he thought.

A pesky deer fly was about to land on Andrea. Jake put his hand out as a sacrifice, let it land, and then hit it with his hat. "You owe me one," he said softly. "I wish I could take you with me when I leave." He sighed. "But that's about as likely as me taking the lake and mountain too."

Andrea was different than the young women he'd worked with on *Wheels*. The young actresses he had met were all mostly obsessed with their appearance and worked hard to market their best feature. Many of them worked with modeling agencies, and they specialized in hair or eyes or body shape. He'd even met one girl who told him she made a lot of money having her hands photographed for magazine layouts. For the most part, the young women he'd met were almost desperate to be noticed, and they constantly dieted and worked out to enhance their appearance. Jake saw none of that desperation in Andrea. For some reason, she seemed comfortable with who she was. She had gone down to the lake after breakfast and washed her face, but she hadn't put on any makeup. It didn't matter. She still looked wonderful. Jake couldn't imagine any of the girls from *Wheels* having enough self-confidence to go anywhere without getting made-up.

He picked some of the flowers and carefully tucked their stems in her hair, amusing himself by seeing how many he could do without waking her. While he was placing the flowers, he spoke softly to her. "You want to know a secret? A few more days and I'd have a tough time leaving you. I've never been in love before. Maybe this is what it's like. Are you surprised? I am. I mean, you're Mountain Woman, for crying out loud. It's like dating George of the Jungle's sister."

The sun was in her face. He moved a little to give her some shade. You know how in *Groundhog Day* Bill Murray had to live the same day over and over again? Well, if I had my choice, this'd be the day I'd choose. There's never going to be another day like this for me.

"Let's pretend you're Snow White, and I'm the prince. A wicked witch has cast an evil spell on you, but if I kiss you, then you'll wake up. Okay?"

He leaned over to kiss her lightly on the lips but then stopped. "It won't work, will it? If I kiss you, you'll wake up all mad at me. You'll tell me we're cousins. And, the thing is, I won't be able to tell you we aren't."

From down by the lake, Vernon called and waved to them.

Jake woke Andrea up. "It looks like your dad's ready to go now," he said.

As she sat up, some of the flowers fell from her hair. She reached up and felt for the others dangling about her face. "What's this all about?"

"Gosh, I don't know. I was sleeping the whole time. You

know what? I bet a flower-elf came while we were sleeping. That happens a lot out here, you know."

"I didn't know that," she said.

"Oh, yeah. Did you have a good nap?"

"I did. And you?"

He gave her a big smile. "I had a great time."

She fixed the flowers in her hair more securely. "I can see that."

"I enjoy nature's beauty—especially you."

"I smell like a campfire."

"I like that in a woman. In fact, I like everything about you. Youda woman!"

She got the same worried look she'd had the night before. "Jake, we need to talk. About last night . . . and about us."

He waved her off. "Look, you don't need to say anything. I've thought about it, and I agree with you that what happened last night isn't right. Sorry. It won't happen again."

"You understand then?" she asked.

"Of course. It's okay for cousins to be close . . . you know, the best of friends. But, like you said, we need to be careful it doesn't go beyond that."

She gave a sigh of relief. "I'm glad you agree. I feel so much better now. We can still have a good time, though, right?"

"Oh, sure, absolutely."

At camp, they rolled up their sleeping bags and took the tent down. Then they packed up and started the long hike back to the car.

Jake was still the slowest hiker, but he didn't mind. Following Andrea and her dad from a distance gave him a chance to think about leaving the next morning. He wasn't sure if he'd tell Andrea the truth or not. The simplest thing for him would be just to walk out, with her thinking they were cousins. She'd find out soon enough that he wasn't who she thought.

He'd postponed telling her the truth because of wanting to spend more time with her. But now he was torn. Every moment with her was precious to him. But, also, every minute he continued this charade made it more likely she'd end up hating him for deceiving her.

One thing was sure. He was not leaving without his cashier's check. *How can I get my money back today without telling her the truth until I leave in the morning?*

When he finally came up with a way, it seemed almost too easy.

* * * * *

After an hour Andrea dropped back to walk with him. "How you doing back here?"

"Not bad at all. Where's your dad?"

"He went ahead. He wanted to talk to a friend of his and get some gas. He'll meet us where we parked the car."

"I've been trying to come up with a way to tell you how I feel about you. I think I've got it. You want to hear it?"

She got that *C'mon,-Jake,-we're-cousins* look again. Then she said, "I don't know. I guess."

"Our friendship is like a glacier."

"You mean because it's pure and clean?"

"No, because it's slow moving and crushes everything in its path."

The sound of her laughter rang through the woods.

He didn't know how to take her laughter. "What?" he said.

She could see he was hurt. "I'm sorry, Jake. I guess I don't know what to make of us." She grew serious and was quiet for a minute, then she looked into his eyes and said, "I've been thinking about you. When we first met, you said

88

you wanted to learn to be more like me. Do you still feel that way?"

He gave her a weak smile. "It comes and goes."

"Well, here's one thing that might help you. When I wake up in the morning, I say a little prayer that I'll be able to help someone that day."

"That doesn't surprise me."

"Helping others is what life's all about." She took his hand. "It's been so great having you here. I don't know what I'd have done without you."

"I've enjoyed it too."

"My dad says you're thinking of leaving tomorrow."

"That's right."

They stopped walking and looked into each other's eyes. "I'm really going to miss you," he said.

"I'll miss you too." She forced a smile, then, not trusting herself, hiked faster. When she was far enough away, she stopped and turned to face him. "Grampa always used to say that someday I'd meet a guy who'd turn my world upside down." She paused. "He just never said it'd be my cousin."

"We'll always have Harrison Lake." He wondered if she'd recognize that he'd borrowed the line from the movie *Casablanca*. She didn't. Apparently she didn't watch as many movies as he did.

"Jake, they'll be reading Grampa's will tomorrow. Is there any chance you can stay an extra day?"

He sighed. "Sorry. I'd like to, but I'd better not."

When they reached the river, they took off their boots and socks. "It might be better if we hold hands while we're crossing," she said.

He smiled. "I'm sure it'll be better."

She started to blush. "I meant safer."

"I know. Just kidding."

His feet were tender, and walking on the slippery rocks was painful. All the way across, he kept saying, "Ouch." He noticed that Andrea wasn't complaining and said to her, "Doesn't it hurt your feet?"

"Sure, but women tolerate pain better than men."

"That can't be true. Ouch!"

"If men had babies, no family would ever have more than one child."

"I don't even want to think about that," he said with a grimace.

"I rest my case."

On the other side, they sat down, dried their feet, and put on their socks and boots. Then they walked across the highway to the parking area. They sat down in the shade of a tree and shared a candy bar.

"You think you might come back here to see . . . us . . . sometime?" she asked.

"Well, to be honest, probably not."

She seemed hurt by his answer. "Sure, there's no reason, really, why you should."

"It'd never be the same," he said. "In fact, in a few days you might not even like me."

"You're crazy if you think that."

She was sitting on the ground, leaning back against a tree. She removed her baseball cap and set it on her backpack. Her shirttail was out; her face was still flushed from the hike; and her hair was matted-down from wearing a baseball cap most of the day.

And he loved it all.

"Is it that bad?" she said, aware of his attention.

"Yeah, it is. In fact, I can hardly stand to look at you."

"I can believe that."

"Just kidding. You know I love that all-natural-ingredients face of yours, don't you?"

She shook off the compliment. "Tell me what it was like fishing this morning."

"You know I don't want to talk about that."

She crumpled the candy wrapper into a wad and stuck it in her jeans pocket and then faced him straight on. "All right, Jake. What *do* you want to talk about?"

"Why are you so different from any other girl I've ever known? Is it the fresh air and the mountains? Is it growing up in a small town? What is it?"

She shrugged her shoulders. "I don't know. I never think of myself as being different."

Because he didn't trust himself to be looking into her eyes, he picked up a pinecone, stood up, and lobbed it into the woods. "You want to know what worries me? That I'll go the rest of my life looking for someone just like you, but I'll never find her."

"Jake, please . . . we've already . . . "

He threw a pinecone as hard as he could, then turned to face her. "No! Just this once, let me say what's in my heart. I'll never find another girl like you. And years from now, I'll look back and realize these last few days we've had together were the best part of my life."

With tears in her eyes, she shook her head. "This isn't doing either one of us any good."

"Look, this isn't about us, okay? I mean it is, but not really. Because I've given up on that. I know there's no hope for us. . . . " He sighed and said more softly, "I know that even more than you do."

"We'll always be cousins."

"Yeah, right," he answered, sarcastically. "What is it about you? I've known a lot of girls in my life, but none of them are like you."

"What's different about me?"

"I don't know. Everything, I guess."

"That doesn't give me much to go on."

Jake thought about it. "You seem more . . . well . . . at peace with yourself."

"I guess what I am comes from my beliefs."

91

"What do you believe that makes you the way you are?" he asked.

"It's hard to say in a few words."

Jake spotted Vernon's car pulling into the parking lot. "Here comes your dad. Tell me something at least."

She stood and brushed the pine needles off her seat. "I know that God loves me." She patted him on the back. "He loves you too, Jake."

"I believe the part about him loving you, but I'm not sure about him loving me."

"He does, though." She looked into his eyes. "I'll always believe that."

He wondered what she would think of him after he was gone, after she found out he wasn't really her cousin. "Always is a long time," he said, just before Vernon pulled up to take them home.

* * * * *

At supper, they had a good time relating their adventures to Andrea's mom. She was a wonderful listener. Her speech was sprinkled with phrases like, "Oh, my gosh! You must have been so surprised."

Jake noticed how many times Andrea touched her mom, either on the hand or on the shoulder, as she passed by. When they first got home, Andrea had greeted her mom with a big hug. That was foreign to Jake; he never hugged his mother. *The way they all relate to each other is so good,* he thought.

Andrea and her parents were so open and so easy to be with that there were moments when he felt like he belonged there. But then he'd think about the deception he was continuing to carry off and feel guilty. To excuse himself, he rationalized: *This isn't my thing. I need to get to Seattle and deal with Dwight Stone. And I really need to get that cashier's check back before I go.* He didn't much like himself for it, but that was who he was. In the morning he would be gone, but it was painful imagining what Andrea would think when she discovered what a jerk he was.

On the trail Jake had thought of a way to get his cashier's check back without telling her the truth. And now it was time to carry out that plan. No matter how bad it made him feel.

After supper, he helped Andrea wash the dishes, and when they were finished they stepped out on the front porch. She started to say something, but he cut her off.

"I'd like to have that cashier's check back, if that's okay," he said.

In the fading light, she looked surprised, but not offended. "Have you changed your mind?"

"No, not really." He gave her an Antonio grin. "You guess."

Andrea thought about it for a moment and then she had the answer. "You're thinking of giving more, aren't you?"

"Well . . . " he said.

"That's it, isn't it?" she pressed. "See, I know you too well, don't I? But, really, Jake, there's no need to give more."

"I'll tell you what, give me back the cashier's check for fifteen thousand, and I'll replace it with a personal check for twenty thousand dollars."

"No, Jake, that's way too much! I can't let you do that."

He smiled. "Why not? I'm happy to help out the little munchkins at the pool. Besides, I've got plenty of money. Really, I insist."

"How come you have so much money?" she asked.

"Investments," he said. He hated it that he had to lie to her but felt he had no choice.

"Jake, that is so . . ." She looked as though she were going to cry, and he wished he deserved the way she was looking at him.

"You're sure?"

"I'm sure."

Andrea went upstairs, and in a minute came back down with the cashier's check. When she handed it to him, Jake said, "My checkbook is with my things in the cabin. I'll write a check for you tonight and leave it at the cabin for you to pick up anytime it's convenient tomorrow."

The lies were piling up. It was like walking through a minefield. Because his real name was on his personal checks, he couldn't actually give her another check. All he could do was promise. However, just imagining what she would think of him when she learned the truth made him grimace.

"Jake, are you all right?" Andrea asked.

"Yeah, I'm fine," he lied, but he felt like a total jerk. He knew he had to tell her the truth, but he didn't have the courage to do so at the moment. He would tell her though. Tonight. Just before he left. She deserved that much.

At eleven o'clock, Jake reminded Andrea and her parents that he had an early train to catch and asked Vernon for a ride out to the cabin. As reluctant as he was to say good-bye, he was exhausted from the hike and needed to get some sleep.

As he was about to leave the house, Andrea came to the door. "Well, I guess this is good-bye. Thanks for everything, Jake."

Jake wasn't sure what to do, but Andrea made it easy for him. She came into his arms. "You're my favorite cousin," she whispered.

"You're mine too."

He thought about kissing her on the lips, but with her mom standing there and Vernon in the car watching them both, and also because of a guilty conscience, he had plenty of reasons not to. He did brush her forehead with

94

his lips. That seemed like a cousin-safe way to show affection.

"There's something I need to tell you," he said, now finally prepared to tell her the truth.

"It's late and my dad is tired. Call me tomorrow night after you get to Seattle. You can tell me then."

That seemed like an easy way out of an awkward situation. "I will."

"You promise?" she asked.

"I promise."

"All right, I'll look forward to hearing from you."

He and Vernon said nothing during the short ride to the cabin, but as they pulled up in front, Vernon said, "We've enjoyed having you here."

"Thank you for everything. I really enjoyed going fishing with you."

"Come back anytime and we'll do it again," Vernon said.

"I'd like that."

They shook hands.

"You want a ride to the station tomorrow?" Vernon asked.

"No, I'd rather walk, but thanks anyway."

And then Vernon was gone.

Jake went in the cabin and got ready for bed. When he was done in the bathroom, he noticed a book on a shelf like the one in Andrea's room. It was also well marked. He turned the pages of the Book of Mormon and read a few random passages that someone had highlighted.

One, in particular, caught his interest.

For behold, this life is the time for men to prepare to meet God; yea, behold the day of this life is the day for men to perform their labors. And now, as I said unto you before, as ye have had so many witnesses, therefore, I beseech of you that ye do not procrastinate the day of your repentance until the end; for after this day of life, which is given us to prepare for eternity, behold, if we do not improve our time while in this life, then cometh the night of darkness wherein there can be no labor performed.

That was a scary thought, and it made him think about the way he had lived his life. He felt guilty, but it also made him a little mad. Who had the right to tell him how to live his life? At the same time, sitting there alone in the night, he had to admit that he had lived a pretty shallow existence. What had he done to prepare himself to meet God? It was not a comfortable thing to consider. He'd wasted a lot of time on things that didn't really matter.

He turned out the light and got into bed. But, like an echo from a mountain canyon, the passage, *This life is the time for men to prepare to meet God,* wouldn't go away.

What have I done to prepare to meet God? I've deceived the only girl I've ever loved. How pleased can God be about that? He punched the pillow with his fist. *I'm going to tell her tomorrow night on the phone.*

His conscience ripped him. *Youda man? Ha! She deserves to hear the truth from you face-to-face. Not over the phone. You order pizza over the phone, for crying out loud. If you're going to admit you're a liar and a cheat, do it to her face.*

He thought about going back and waking Andrea and her folks and telling them the truth. He might even have done that, but then he thought of another possibility. Maybe he could persuade Christopher to stay an extra day. After the reading of the will, he'd tell Andrea and her parents the truth. Then he and Christopher could leave for Seattle.

This new plan cheered him up and made it possible for him to fall asleep.

* * * * *

For the second day in a row, Jake got up early. His plan was to try to talk Christopher into staying an extra day, but if he refused, Jake decided he could call Andrea while on the train.

So you might not tell her the truth face-to-face? he asked himself.

It depends on what Christopher wants to do.

Why does it depend on Christopher? Why doesn't anything depend on you? Why don't you take responsibility for the things you do that are wrong?

What does it matter? She's going to end up hating me either way.

On his way out, he picked up an empty plastic flowerpot from the porch.

When he came to the meadow of wild flowers, he transplanted one of the small flowers into the pot and continued on his way. He wanted to take it home as a souvenir.

Jake was waiting as the Amtrak passenger train heading for Seattle came to a stop. The conductor placed the step on the ground for passengers, and Christopher got off the train. He looked even more frazzled than usual.

"You ready? Let's go." Christopher noticed the flowerpot. "What's that?"

"A mountain flower. They grow all around here."

Christopher scowled at the wilted, anemic-looking flower. "Look, do yourself a favor and dump it. It'll never survive the trip."

Assuming that Jake was right behind him, Christopher got back on board the train. He was all business. "I can't believe it. I leave you for two days and you turn into a gardener?"

Still standing on the platform, Jake glanced down at the flower. It was already beginning to die. "Do you have an actual appointment with Dwight Stone?" he asked.

Christopher turned from the top of the train steps. "No, he won't return my calls anymore. We'll just have to camp out at his office until he'll talk to us."

"So there's a chance we'll go out there and not even meet with him for a couple of days?"

Christopher looked down at Jake and clenched his teeth. "What are you saying?"

"Stay here one more day with me. You could meet Andrea."

Christopher got off the train and approached Jake. "Absolutely not! I can't believe you! Do you have any idea what Dwight Stone can do for us?"

"I'm just talking one more day for the reading of her grandfather's will. We can stay at a cabin by the lake. It'll give you a chance to relax."

The conductor reached down to place the portable stair back onto the train.

"All aboard!"

Christopher was yelling at him. "Relax! You want me to relax?"

"Look around this place. I mean, it's so beautiful. Can't you see that?" Jake asked.

"Listen to me! Right now everything I've ever wanted in my entire life is wrapped up in Dwight Stone! And you want me to stay here and look at chipmunks? What's the matter with you, anyway?"

Jake looked down at the wilted mountain flower he held in his hands.

"You really don't care what I want out of life, do you?" Christopher yelled.

"Of course I care, but what difference is one day going to make?"

"How should I know? It could make all the difference in the world, but we won't know unless we go out there."

The conductor called out to them. "We're ready to go."

"You said you'd go with me *today*," Christopher complained.

"I know, but I have to stay one more day. I'll catch up with you tomorrow."

"If you won't help me when I need it, then you can just forget the whole thing!" Christopher knocked the flowerpot out of Jake's hand. The soil and the flower lay scattered on the ground.

Christopher took one last parting shot before getting on the train. "The truth is, Jake, I never could count on you for anything."

Jake watched as the train pulled out of the station, then got down on his knees and gathered up the soil and the flower and carefully put it all back in the pot.

7

The first thing Jake did after leaving the train station was replant the mountain flower in the place where he'd dug it up. Then he walked to the cabin and slept.

A couple of hours later he returned to Andrea's house. He went around to the back and knocked on the kitchen door.

Marilyn answered it. "Jake, how nice! I thought you were leaving today."

"I decided to stay for the reading of the will."

"I'm glad you did. Come in. Have you had breakfast?"

"Not really."

"Good, let me go tell Andrea you're here. She'll be so happy you decided to stay."

Jake couldn't hear what Marilyn said upstairs, but he did hear Andrea's reaction. "Are you serious? He's still here?"

Andrea, barefoot, wearing loosely fitting blue-plaid pajamas, bounded down the stairs, and ran into the kitchen. She skidded to a stop.

"Well, hi," she said, waving tentatively.

"Hi, yourself." He smiled.

They stared at each other, not knowing what to say. Finally, Jake broke the silence.

"Nice pj's," he teased.

Andrea blushed. "I'll go get dressed," she said, then smiled, "Don't go away." She backed out of the kitchen and disappeared into the hall, then she stuck her head back in the entryway.

"Not that it's any business of yours, but I sleep with the window open. It gets cold here at night, even in the summer." And then she left.

When are you going to tell her the truth? he asked himself as he sat at the kitchen table, waiting for her to come back.

I'll tell her tonight.

Tell her now.

No.

Why not?

I want as much time as I can have with her.

While Marilyn worked in the garden, Jake and Andrea had breakfast together.

What would it be like to do this every day? he thought. *Just the two of us in our own little place. Maybe I'd have an auto shop in town. And maybe someday we'd have kids.*

"What are you thinking about?" she asked.

"Just daydreaming, that's all."

"Must have been a good one. You had a big grin on your face."

"I guess I was thinking about my favorite infomercial."

"Where everybody's happy?"

His smile vanished. "Yeah . . . where everybody's happy."

He tapped his forehead with his hand. "Oh, rats. I left your check at the cabin. How about if we get it later?"

"Sure, no problem," she said.

After breakfast Jake helped Vernon set up some extra chairs in the living room for the reading of the will.

At ten-thirty that morning, family members gathered in the living room to hear Mr. Baird, a local attorney, read the will. It was a formal occasion and Jake and Andrea dressed up. Jake wore Grampa's suit again and Andrea wore a church dress.

The two of them sat in back, near the door to the kitchen.

"And to Andrea, I bequeath my cabin near the lake. Andrea, no matter where you end up, I hope that, at least once a year, you'll bring your family to the cabin."

"We got the cabin!" Andrea excitedly whispered in Jake's ear.

"*You* got the cabin."

"You can use it anytime you want."

"Thanks."

The reading of the will took a long time, and it was tedious to Jake.

"And to our neighbor's boy, Jeffrey Wills, I leave my new, self-propelled lawnmower. Jeffrey, take good care of it, change the oil every twenty hours of operation, and, who knows, you could earn enough money for college."

Jake sat there for as long as he could stand it and then slipped into the kitchen. He found a cookie jar full of molasses cookies on the counter and a half-gallon jug of milk in the fridge. To pass the time, he thumbed mindlessly through a gardening magazine.

Two cookies later, Andrea came in to check on him.

She scowled. "Those were Grampa's favorite cookies." She said it like he had just bulldozed a family shrine.

"I can see why. Want one?"

"No thanks."

"I think Grampa probably would want us to enjoy his cookies, don't you?" he said.

She sighed. "Maybe so." She sat down. She picked up a cookie and took a tiny bite.

Jake got up from the table, got another glass, and poured

it full of milk for Andrea. As he set it down in front of her, he rested his hand on her shoulder.

"Like they say, death is just a door."

She nodded. "I know, but it still doesn't make it easy to have him gone."

"You've lost someone you loved very much."

She touched the back of her neck and grimaced.

"You okay?" he asked.

"Just a tension headache, that's all. I don't know why. I guess it's all of Grampa's things being given away. It seems so final."

"When my mom is under a lot of stress, she has me massage her neck and shoulders. I'm very good at it. So, if you want me to . . . "

"Well, I don't know . . . "

"You trust me, don't you?" The minute he said it, he regretted it, knowing she had no reason to trust him.

"I guess it'd be all right," she said.

The massage Jake had learned from his mom consisted of tiny little karate chops to the muscles.

"That feels *so* good," she said. The chopping action made her sound like a talking helicopter when she spoke. She reached for a cookie and took a big bite. "This has been a hard summer. I'll be ready when it's time to go back to school."

"Where do you go to school?"

"Rick's College." At least that's how it sounded to Jake.

"Who's Rick, and why does he have a college?"

"You've heard of Ricks College, haven't you?" she asked.

"Hey, I'm from back East. I can't keep track of every podunk college in Montana."

"It's in Idaho."

"Sorry . . . every podunk college in Idaho."

She turned around and glared at him. "*Podunk* college?"

"Right, let me guess. It's in the back of Rick's Curio Shop, right? The way Rick works it, each student is assigned to make little knickknacks for the tourists."

"For your information, Ricks College is the largest private two-year college in the United States."

"Yeah, right. So what are you majoring in? Plastic bears?"

"Very funny, Jake, very funny."

"I'm serious. What are you studying in school?"

"Music."

"That makes sense. You have a nice voice."

"My mom says you're studying to be an accountant, is that right?"

"Numbers are my life," Jake said, wondering what else she might know about the real Cameron.

"Sounds boring."

"To some people it might be, but not to me." Jake wondered if he was going overboard.

She looked over her shoulder at him. "Can you do my back too?"

The way she used her folded arms as a pillow for her head reminded Jake of when he was in kindergarten, and it was naptime.

They heard the doorbell ring but paid no attention to it.

They were, of course, just a few feet from grieving family members and friends. "Actually . . . this might not be the best time for this," he said.

"It's okay."

He started his karate chop massage on her upper back.

A minute later her mom and dad and several family members burst into the kitchen.

"Andrea!" Marilyn asked. "What are you doing?"

Andrea quickly stood up. "I asked Jake to massage my back. It's okay, though, because we're cousins."

"Cousins, are you?" Marilyn glared at Jake, then reached behind her into the dining room. "Cameron, would you come in here, please?"

A tall young man on crutches hobbled into the room.

Marilyn continued. "Andrea, this is your cousin Cameron. He just arrived. He would've been here earlier, but he had an accident and landed in the hospital."

"I thought everybody knew what happened," Cameron said. "I called and talked to Uncle Albert."

"You talked to Uncle Albert?" Marilyn asked.

"Yes."

"Well, that's very interesting," Marilyn said. "Uncle Albert has been dead for two years."

All eyes in the room turned to Jake. "It's a miracle," he said weakly, knowing he was busted.

"Did you talk to Cameron on the phone?" Marilyn asked Jake.

"Yeah, I did, actually. He called just before the funeral. There was nobody else around to get it."

Andrea approached him. Her face was a mask of astonishment. "If you're not Cameron, who are you?"

This was not going to be fun. He took a deep breath, then said, "My name is Jake Petricelli. I'm from Chicago. I got off the train by mistake. The whole thing is a big misunderstanding."

"But you . . . and me . . . we . . . "

"I know. The reason we got along so well at first is . . . well, because, I thought I was dead."

"Dead!"

"Yes. You see, I saw the light."

"What light?" she asked.

"Well, of course, now I know it was the light of a train going by. That was after I knocked myself out."

"You knocked yourself out?" she asked.

"Not on purpose. I was hungry."

"You knock yourself out when you're hungry?" Andrea asked.

"Actually, this may be a little hard to explain."

105

She seemed to be in shock. "You're not a part of the family, though?"

"No."

"And you didn't come here to go to Grampa's funeral?"

"No, I'm on my way to Seattle."

"So you lied to me from the beginning, didn't you?"

"Not at first. But, later, I guess I did. Sorry. I was going to tell you today."

"What about the twenty thousand dollars you promised to help keep the pool open?" Andrea asked.

This was going to be harder than he had ever imagined. "Well, actually . . . " He took a deep breath . . . "that's not going to happen." He spoke so softly it was barely audible. He tried to think of what he could say that would soften the blow. If he could just let Andrea know what she'd come to mean to him; if he could just take away the profound shock and pain he saw in her eyes.

Vernon seemed more disappointed than angry. "We trusted you," he said.

"I know you did. You treated me very well. I'm sorry."

Her eyes brimming with tears, Andrea turned away and walked out of the room.

"If you have any trouble with him, call me," Vernon said to Marilyn. "I'm going to see how Andrea is doing."

Jake moved toward the back door.

"Not so fast!" Marilyn called out. "You're not leaving here wearing my father's suit. You probably have in mind walking off with it, don't you?"

"No. Look, my clothes are at the cabin. I'll leave the suit there."

"Why should we trust you, after all the lies you've told us? I will not have you stealing my dad's perfectly good suit."

"No offense, Ma'am, but if you'll just think about what you're saying . . . "

She called out. "Vernon, please come down here right away!"

Jake didn't want to deal with Vernon again. "Fine, then, lady! Have it your way!"

While Andrea's mother stared at him in astonishment, Jake ripped off Grampa's suit coat, tie, white shirt, and trousers and left them in a pile on the kitchen floor.

Even though he was wearing only boxer shorts and shoes and socks, he was so mad that he marched into the living room, past the attorney and the family members still gathered there, and out the front door.

Andrea saw him leave the house from her upstairs bedroom. She opened the window, leaned out, and yelled, "What are you doing out there like that?"

"This is not my fault! Your mom told me to take off the suit, and when I didn't, she called for your dad."

"She was calling my dad so he could drive you to Grampa's cabin so you could change."

Jake felt foolish. He cleared his throat. "Oh."

"Come back in the house and put something on. You can't be out there like that."

"You're crazy if you think I'm coming back there!"

"You're calling *me* crazy? I'm not the one standing outside in my underwear!"

He started to walk away.

"Jake!"

He stopped and turned around.

"I wish I'd never met you!"

He closed his eyes to try to shut out the pain. "You're the lucky one then," he said softly, then turned and started walking toward the cabin.

A minute later a sheriff's car approached. When it got alongside Jake, it slowed down. The officer driving the car was wearing dark glasses, but his mouth looked as though he was not amused.

107

Jake looked down at his boxer shorts. He hoped that they might pass for jogging shorts. The dark socks and dress shoes he was wearing kind of ruined the illusion, but he started jogging.

With the sheriff's car keeping pace, Jake jogged for a half block. Finally he looked over at the policeman and waved. The deputy gave a stiff little salute and drove off. A few minutes later Jake reached the cabin.

* * * * *

There was a light rain and it had gotten chilly as he walked back to town. The mountain flowers had closed their petals to protect themselves from the cold.

Jake approached the ticket counter at the tiny one-room train station. "I need a ticket."

The ticket agent, in his mid-sixties, looked up from a crossword puzzle. "Where to?"

Jake shook his head. "I don't know."

"You have to know where you're going before I can issue you a ticket."

"You think I don't know that?" Jake raged.

"Hey, You don't have to yell. Where do you want to go?"

Jake turned and walked out of the station.

He decided to take a walk to clear his head and after a time, he ended up at the city park. He spotted the swimming pool and went over to it. There was a sign posted on the gate. It read: "Closed for the Season."

Jake stood at the chainlink fence and stared vacantly at the empty pool that had once been full of water and kids. He wondered how often Andrea had prayed that the pool wouldn't close. But it had. So what good were all her prayers?

Every day she says a prayer that she'll be able to help someone, he thought. *I'm not like that. I only think of myself.*

Ask anyone. Ask Christopher. Ask Natasha. Ask Andrea. Ask anyone who's ever known me. They'll all say the same thing. Jake Petricelli is egotistical, shallow, and self-centered. That's what I am and there's no changing it.

Andrea is going to go the rest of her life thinking that everything I said, everything we experienced, was a lie. But it wasn't.

I was dead, and then, with Andrea, I was alive. And now I'm back to being dead again.

Suddenly he realized he wasn't alone. A little blonde girl, maybe six years old, was standing looking up at him. He wiped his eyes and tried to smile. "I'm okay now. Really."

"It's okay. I cried too," she said. She got on her bike and started to ride off.

He called out after her. "You cried because of the pool closing?"

She nodded, then continued on her way.

He walked around the fence surrounding the pool until finally he stood in front of the door to the changing rooms and office. On the door was a notice explaining that the pool would be closed the rest of the summer. It was fastened to the door with tape. But the upper right-hand corner had peeled away from the wood, so the sign was starting to curl. Without really thinking, he pressed it back in place, but, a few seconds later, the tape released, and the sign curled back again.

He pictured Andrea, wearing those baggy pajamas, kneeling by her bed, praying that the pool would stay open. He would never see her again. And yet she'd given him something he'd never forget. She'd given him, if only for a short time, hope. Hope that he could be a better person than he had been.

He tugged at the bent-over corner of the sign. And then he smiled and pulled the sign completely off the door, tore it into pieces, and threw it in a trash can.

Fifteen minutes later he was in the office of Mr. Stephenson of City Parks and Recreation.

Mr. Stephenson looked at the cashier's check for fifteen thousand dollars Jake had just given him. "Why are you doing this?"

"Why do you care? It's my money, isn't it? Just don't tell Andrea it was me."

When Jake got back to the train station, he told the ticket agent, "I know where I want to go now."

8

Once again on the train bound for Seattle, Jake went to the dome car. He found an empty seat near the rear of the car, pulled out his cell phone, and called Christopher.

"Yeah?" Christopher said glumly.

"Christopher? It's me. I'm on my way."

"Don't bother."

"What do you mean?"

"Stone's not talking to anyone. His secretary told me that his wife left him and that he's in major depression. She says he's just sitting in his office, staring at his wife's picture. I've been waiting outside his office all day. It's a waste of time for you to come out here."

"I'm coming anyway. We'll find a way, Christopher."

"What about that girl you were seeing?"

Jake sighed. "It's over."

"For good?"

"Yeah."

"It's just as well. We'll find plenty of chicks once we sign a deal with Dwight Stone."

"I'll never find anyone like her."

Two days later, at seven-fifteen in the morning, Jake and Christopher were sitting on a large piece of driftwood on a rocky beach on the shore of Puget Sound, near Seattle.

111

Above them, on top of a wooded hill, stood Dwight Stone's mansion. A chatty clerk in a convenience store had told them Dwight Stone took a walk along this beach every morning.

"I'd better not let him see me," Christopher said, hugging his clipboard for comfort.

"Why not?"

"He knows what I look like. Two nights ago, when he got in his car after work, I ran after him, trying to get him to talk to me."

Jake smiled. "You're such a smoothie. Okay, I'll talk to him."

Christopher moved off, into the pine forest, out of sight.

A few minutes later Jake saw a lone figure coming down a steep walkway from the large house and onto the beach. Jake waited until the man was about to pass him.

"Mr. Stone, I'm Jake Petricelli. You know, from *Wheels?*"

Stone wheeled around to face Jake. "You're with the psychopath, right?"

"I admit Christopher can be a little intense at times."

"A little intense? He chased me through the parking lot and out into the street. Almost caught up with me at a stoplight. Just kept running . . . "

"He's really quite harmless. In fact, he's around here somewhere."

Stone looked around wildly, then began to retreat toward his house.

"Look, if you could just give me five minutes of your time," Jake said, walking to catch up with him.

"You get no time. Do you want me to have you both arrested?"

Jake tried to hand him the videotape. "Please, just look at this. That's all I'm asking."

Stone shook his head and walked faster. "Forget it. You had your chance, and you blew it."

Jake stepped in front of Stone, blocking his path.

112

"Get out of my way!"

"I'm not asking for me, but for Christopher. I feel bad about him missing maybe his one and only shot."

Dwight shook his head and stepped around Jake, who dropped his hands to his side and let him go.

"Mr. Stone, I know you don't care, but I just lost the only woman I'll ever love."

Stone took two more steps, then stopped. He turned around. "Can't you go back to her?"

"No, it's too late for that now."

Stone stared vacantly at the waves washing up on the rocky shore. "It happens."

They stood there for a long time. Then, without looking back at Jake, Stone extended his hand. "Give me the tape," he said. "Stay here. I'll be back after I've watched it."

Jake walked along the beach, thinking about Andrea and how much he missed her.

An hour later Stone came back. He handed Jake the videotape.

"Well, what did you think?" Jake asked.

"It's way beyond awful."

"All of it?"

Stone paused. "I liked the cars."

So that was it. One more dream dashed to pieces. "Thanks, anyway." Jake started to leave.

"Where are you going?" Stone asked.

"You just said you didn't like it."

"That's way too kind. The fact is, I hated it."

"You want me to stick around so you can tell me how much you hated it?"

"No, I have something else in mind for you," Stone said.

"What? Your car won't start?"

"I want you to do a movie with me. You ever hear of James Dean?"

"Oh, yeah, sure."

"I want to do a remake of his movie, *Giant*. I can see you in the lead role. You interested?"

Jake swallowed. "Maybe. But you don't get me unless Christopher is involved in the picture, as . . . a, some kind of assistant director."

"I don't do business that way," Stone said.

"And I don't abandon my friends." Jake turned to leave.

He'd taken ten steps when Stone called out after him. "What I meant was I don't *usually* do business that way."

Jake stopped and turned around. "You'll make an exception this time?"

"You're too pushy," Stone said, gruffly.

"Probably," Jake nodded. He couldn't suppress a grin. "When do we start?"

"I'm having a few friends in tonight. People in the business. I'd like you . . . and the other guy . . . to meet them."

Jake put his fingers to his mouth and whistled, and Christopher came running out of the woods, carrying his clipboard.

"Is he any good?" Stone asked.

"He's very talented. You won't be sorry. He's very good with details."

A sudden gust of wind caught the clipboard, and some of the notes were blown away. Christopher scurried around, desperately trying to retrieve them.

Dwight Stone shook his head. "Very good with details, huh? I can see that."

* * * * *

By nine o'clock that night, Dwight Stone's house was crammed with beautiful, talented, creative people.

While Christopher worked at charming two good-looking wannabe actresses with his wit, Jake stared at some

114

hydrangeas the florist had brought. The blossoms came in gaudy, soccer-ball sized clumps.

Dwight Stone entered the room and walked to where Jake was standing. "Come with me," he demanded.

Stone stepped up onto the raised hearth of a large natural-stone fireplace. He motioned Jake to stand beside him. "This is Jake Petricelli," he announced. "He'll be taking the role of James Dean in our remake of *Giant.*"

There was only polite applause because most of the men in the group thought they should have been chosen for the part.

"Show 'em your abs," Stone said to Jake. "Take off your shirt."

"I'd rather not."

"Don't be ridiculous." Stone addressed the group: "I want you all to see this. Jake?"

Jake looked at the crowd of beautiful people, all staring at him. Then he slowly took off his shirt.

"And turn to the left . . . and turn to the right . . . and back to the center," Stone coached. "And . . . turn around."

His face flushed with embarrassment, Jake did as Stone instructed.

"That's it. Show's over," Stone said with a smile.

Just then, someone announced that Clayton Broderick, the renowned British actor, had just showed up. Stone and the others ran to meet him, leaving Jake alone.

Jake felt sick. Fighting nausea, he ran for the nearest bathroom. He ran water over his face, then dried himself, but decided to stay near the bathroom just in case the nausea returned.

There were two doors into the bathroom. Jake opened the other door, and found himself in a large bedroom. He went in and sat down on the bed and waited for his stomach to settle.

Sitting on the night table next to the bed there was a

framed photograph of Dwight Stone, a pretty woman, and a little girl, maybe nine or ten years old. Jake assumed the woman was Stone's wife. There was something about her that reminded him of Andrea. He picked up the picture and looked more closely. It wasn't the hair. This woman had sun-bleached blonde hair while Andrea's was brown. Feature by feature, Jake tried to decide what it was about this woman that reminded him of Andrea.

Finally it came to him. The similarity was the lack of posing, the absence of trying to be impressive—that was the connection. While Dwight Stone was demanding the camera pay attention to him, this woman stood to the side and a little behind her famous husband. Looking at her, it was easy for Jake to imagine that she was content to be home with her daughter, away from the lights and fame and misplaced glory.

And now she's left him, he thought, remembering what Christopher had said.

He might have stayed there the rest of the evening, but people kept coming through the bedroom on their way to the bathroom. "Is someone in there?" one woman asked.

"No."

"Oh, I thought you were waiting . . . "

"No, I was just sitting here, but I'm leaving now."

He didn't want to talk to anyone. He was ashamed he'd let Dwight Stone parade him around with his shirt off. He wasn't sure why he'd gone along with it, except for the fact he hadn't wanted to disappoint Stone in front of his friends. *He used me,* he thought, *to demonstrate his power.*

Jake spent the rest of the evening on the veranda sitting in a lounge chair, watching through a window the swirl of activity going on inside. Seated off to the side on the darkened deck, Jake was out of the way and hidden from view, which was what he wanted. Everyone seemed content to ignore him. He was a newcomer and had no power. Also, he was a threat to everyone if Dwight decided to favor him.

116

Jake soon realized that the veranda was the place where battle plans were being laid. "Have you talked to Dwight about your screenplay?" a charming woman asked her equally charming husband.

"Not yet. I can never get him alone. What about you?"

"No. Clayton Broderick's showing up here ruined everything. It was better when Vera was here. I could always talk to her."

"Talk to Rachel then."

"I doubt Rachel was even invited. Dwight won't bring her out in public until after the divorce." The couple left the veranda and stepped back into the brightly lighted house, returning to the battle.

Jake laid his head back on the lounge chair and looked up at the stars. *What will I be like in twenty years?* he thought. *Rich? Powerful? Or bowing and scraping before someone like Dwight Stone, trying to talk him into throwing me a bone? Will I be on my second marriage, or my fourth? Or will I still be married but seeing someone on the side?*

He watched as Stone and Clayton Broderick entered the main living room. The power base suddenly changed, and everyone, including Dwight, basked in the brilliance of Britain's most famous actor. Everything Clayton said was greeted by loud laughter as though he were uproariously funny, and people fawned over him continuously.

Half an hour later, after Clayton left, Stone took over again as king of the hill.

The couple who'd met on the veranda finally caught up with Stone. They were close enough for Jake to hear their conversation.

"Charles is working on a new screenplay," his wife said. "I think it's brilliant."

"I'd love to see it sometime," Stone said, then excused himself.

"Should I give the screenplay to him now?" the man asked his wife.

"No, we don't want to look like we're desperate. Wait until next week. Tuesday, I think."

They left again.

I want to be an actor, Jake thought. *And I want to be successful. So why does all this depress me so much?*

At first he had no answer. He was at a party with some of the most talented people in America. And yet, for some reason, it all seemed so artificial and meaningless.

For a time, he thought it was because he kept comparing the women at the party with Andrea. Some of the dresses being worn looked as though the seamstress had run out of fabric. Everywhere he looked, Jake saw bare backs, bare midriffs, and plunging necklines.

Some of the older women looked as though they were walking commercials for the wonders of cosmetic surgery: their tummies tucked, their necks trimmed, their wrinkles zapped by lasers. It was all a little sad. Jake wasn't sure what features they'd been born with and what parts had been added or removed later.

Jake thought about how it had been, being with Andrea. Even while camping, she looked wonderful, and all she had done was run a damp washcloth over her face. For him, her natural beauty was preferable to any of the artificial kind that was so prevalent at the party.

I'll never find anyone like her again, he thought.

However, that wasn't the most depressing thing he was considering. He felt as though he were standing on a beach, watching a tidal wave rushing toward him, knowing that no matter how hard he tried, he'd never be able to outrun it.

These people are going to turn me into one of them, he thought.

That was the thought that terrified him.

* * * * *

At ten-thirty, Jake went to the guest bedroom Christopher and he would be sharing. He watched infomercials until Christopher came in, excited and happy and wanting to talk.

"Everyone loves me here!" he said. "All I have to say is, 'I'm going to be Dwight's assistant on his next movie,' and, I swear, they fall all over me, wanting me to talk to Dwight about this or that. Even the chicks love me."

"I'm glad you're having a good time," Jake said glumly.

"What's eating you?"

"Nothing, nothing at all. Everything's just great."

"Don't give me that. What's wrong?"

At first Jake didn't even know how to begin. And then he thought of a movie analogy. "You've seen *Wizard of Oz*, right?"

"Yeah, sure, why?"

"The Tin Man had no heart, the Scarecrow had no brains, and the Lion had no courage. I should've been there with 'em."

"How come?"

"I have no convictions."

"What are you talking about?"

"I just go along with what people want me to do. That's not right."

"So? If it gets you where you want to go, what's the harm?"

"No, you've got to have a foundation, you've got to have standards, you've got to have a base."

"Where do you get this stuff anyway? Who you been talking to?"

Jake shook his head, went to the window, and watched the surf surge onto the rocks.

"It's that chick from Montana, isn't it? I thought it was all over between you two."

"It is," Jake said

"Get over it then. Move on. Find someone else."

Jake shook his head. "I can't."

"What, are you crazy? Did you even *look* at the foxes here tonight?"

"This is not about finding a girl for me, okay?" Jake snapped.

"What's it about then?"

Jake turned around. "I don't know."

"You're just tired. I'm going to take a shower and then go to bed. I've got to be fresh for the morning. I've got a date to play tennis with last year's Miss . . . Georgia, Tennessee, South Carolina . . . I'm not exactly sure, but it's definitely one of the southern states."

"You don't play tennis."

Christopher gave a low rumbling laugh. "I do now!"

While Christopher was taking a shower, Jake turned off the lights and sat on a chair on the balcony outside his room and watched the waves.

Just after Christopher went to bed, Jake decided he needed to talk. He pulled up a chair next to Christopher's bed. "The thing is, I know what it feels like to die and look back on a life that's had no direction or purpose," he said. "I read something the other day that keeps coming back to me. It said this life is the time for men to prepare to meet God. You ever think about things like that?"

Christopher rolled over so his back was to Jake. "Right now, this is the time for me to prepare to meet Miss Georgia Peach . . . or Miss Florida Key. Man, I wish I could remember. But whatever she is, she needs me to be in top form on the court tomorrow."

Jake gave up and went back out on the balcony.

* * * * *

It was a long, sleepless night. Finally, around four-thirty, Jake got out of bed and went back on the balcony to watch the waves and the fast-moving dark clouds.

120

An hour later he saw Dwight Stone heading out to take his morning walk along the beach.

A few minutes later Jake caught up with Dwight.

"You're up early," Dwight said.

Jake nodded. "I need to go away for a few days."

"What for?"

"To try one more time with that girl I was telling you about."

"Is she worth it?" Dwight asked.

Jake nodded. "Yeah, she is. When I first met her, I thought she was an angel."

Dwight nodded. "Tell me about it. And then, after a while, she turned into a devil, right?"

Jake shook his head. "No, she stayed the same. I'm the one who changed. I just have to convince her of that."

Dwight nodded. "I'll give you ten days, and then I'll need you back here."

* * * * *

The airline pilots' strike was still in place, so Jake took the Amtrak headed for Chicago. He rode in the dome car. Once they were out of Seattle, he phoned his mother.

"You're going to see a girl who lives on a glacier?" she asked. "Why, Jake? Is it some sort of penance?"

"I think I'm in love."

His mom let out a disappointed sigh. "It's just as well, I guess."

"What do you mean, Mom?"

"A photographer friend of yours visited Natasha last night. She made him pigs in a blanket. They got along very well. He's coming back tonight."

"I'm really glad for her."

"So how does Glacier Girl feel about you?"

"Well, not too good right now. I'm not sure she'll even speak to me."

121

"Don't waste your time with a girl who won't talk to you. You'll get plenty of that once you're married."

* * * * *

Because he'd gotten so little sleep the night before, Jake slept most of the trip, but three hours from West Glacier, he woke up. In the seat in front of him a young mother with a fussy baby and a cranky three-year-old boy was having a tough time. Jake noticed the boy was holding a couple of *Star Wars* action figures.

He knelt in the aisle beside the boy, picked up his Darth Vader action figure, and, using all his acting skills, imitated Darth Vader. The boy smiled. Jake glanced at the aisle seat and then at the woman. She nodded an okay. He sat down, put the boy on his lap, grabbed the Luke Skywalker action figure and the show began.

"Give in to the dark side, Luke," Darth Vader demanded.

"Never," Luke answered.

Suddenly the boy had a big smile on his face.

An hour later the boy was sleeping in Jake's arms. The mother and the baby were also asleep. "Wow, tough audience," Jake said softly to himself.

Montgomery, moving through the dome car, stopped beside Jake. "You still hungry?" he asked with a wide grin.

Jake smiled. "Not as much."

Montgomery placed his broad hand on Jake's shoulder. "Good for you," he said, then continued down the aisle.

* * * * *

Jake was standing at the door as the train slowed down for its West Glacier stop. He was surprised to see Andrea at the station seeing her cousin Cameron off.

Jake waited until Cameron boarded another car on the train, and then he stepped off.

There was Andrea, once again caught in the sun's radiance, looking like an angel, even in jeans and a sweatshirt.

She saw him, let out a little gasp, and then stared at him. It seemed they stood like that forever, but it ended when he took one step in her direction. She shook her head, turned, and walked quickly away.

It was obvious she didn't want to see him. He wasn't sure if he should go after her or get back on the train.

She might have walked out of his life forever if it hadn't been for the noise. Jake and Andrea both turned around. The little boy Jake had played with was banging on the window with his Darth Vader action figure.

Montgomery motioned the mother with the baby and her son to follow him. A few seconds later, they appeared on the steps of the train.

"Thank the nice man for playing with you," the mother prompted the boy.

"T'ank you for p'aying with me!"

"You're welcome!" Jake waved.

The train began to pull away from the station. Jake stood and waved for as long as he could see the little boy. When he turned, Andrea was standing next to him.

They looked into each other's eyes. "I still don't know who you are," she said.

He shrugged his shoulders. "It's pretty much a moving target for me too."

"Why did you come back?"

He struggled for an answer that would keep her from walking away. "Gardening."

"Gardening?"

"Yeah, pretty much."

"I don't understand."

"Let's take a walk and I'll try to explain."

They followed the same route they took the first time they met.

"You were the one who put up the money to keep the pool open, weren't you?" she asked.

"You can't prove that."

"You were though. I'm sure of it."

When they came to the field of flowers, he stopped. "This is what I came back for . . . mountain flowers."

"What about them?"

He touched her chin with his thumb and gently moved her head until they were looking into each other's eyes. "A mountain flower is very beautiful. It does really well up here even though the winters are so hard. At first you'd think it could survive under any conditions, but it can't. It needs certain things in order to do well."

"What does a mountain flower need?" she asked.

"You tell me. You're the mountain flower I came back for."

"Honesty."

He cringed. "You're right. I'm sorry for not being honest with you after I found out I wasn't dead."

"You keep saying you thought you were dead, but it doesn't make sense. How could you think you were dead?"

"You got a minute?"

A light rain began to fall. They stepped under a nearby tree and stood there talking until the shower ended and the sun came out again. Then they continued their walk.

"That's the way it happened," he said.

"That is so weird, but thanks for telling me."

At the pond, he tossed a rock into the water. "You know what? Sometimes, if a frog tries real hard, he can turn into a prince."

She shook her head. "Jake?"

"What?"

She didn't want to hurt his feelings. "Nothing."

124

When they came to where the trail was blocked with snow, he offered to carry her across the snow in his arms, but she had no interest in being physically close to him. She made it across on her own.

Finally they came to the lookout. "Why did you come back?" she asked.

"First of all, to apologize for the way I treated you. I should have told you right away when I realized that I was alive and that we weren't cousins."

"That would've been much better."

"Also, I can't get you out of my mind. I'm different now."

"For the better?"

"I think so."

"I'm glad." She paused. "I prayed for you."

"Thanks. I can use all the prayers I can get right now."

"How come?"

"The other reason I came back is to ask you to marry me," he said.

She stared at him, dumbfounded. "You're right—there is a time warp here."

"It doesn't have to be today."

"Marriage? Are you serious? I don't even know you. And what I do know about you, I don't respect."

"Look, I realize it'll take some time. But that's okay, because I have to leave the country for a while anyway."

"Are you in trouble with the law?" she asked.

"No," he answered curtly, insulted she'd think that.

"Well, how should I know? Why do you have to leave the country?"

"I'm going to make a movie."

"A movie?"

"Yeah. I'm an actor."

"You are?"

"I'm good with cars too. I used to work as a mechanic."

"See, these are all things I would need to know about

125

you if we were to ever get married. You know, in case any-one asked."

"I'll e-mail you my every thought while I'm in Argentina."

"Argentina?"

"That's where the movie will be shot. Are you saying there's a chance we could get married when I come back from Argentina?"

"No, Jake, there isn't. Sorry."

He nodded his head. "Well, okay, I had to ask. How come?"

"When I get married, I want it to be, not just until death, but forever."

"And you can arrange that?" he asked.

"I can . . . in a Mormon temple."

"Look, I'm real close on this one."

"How do you figure that?"

"The first time I met you, I wanted to be with you for-ever, so this isn't that much of a stretch for me."

"You don't even know what Mormons believe."

"I can learn, though, right?"

She shook her head. "It's not that easy."

"Don't give me that, Andrea. You people have mission-aries. Don't deny it. I've seen 'em. They teach people, right? So why can't they teach me?"

She whirled around. "You want the missionaries to teach you?" she asked angrily.

"Sure, why not?"

She threw up her hands. "Fine then! I'll have the missionaries come tonight." She stormed away to the edge of the lookout to get away from him.

"Don't pout, Andrea."

"I'm not pouting!"

"It sure looks like pouting to me."

"How do I know you won't con the missionaries like you

conned me? How do I know I can ever trust anything you say?"

He shook his head. "I guess you don't. You'll just have to give me some time."

She had her arms folded tightly and stood with her back to him.

"I fell in love with you the very first time I saw you," he said. "You really did look like an angel."

"Really? An angel? You mean because I was naive and believed all the lies you dished out?"

"I'm sorry for that. But I can't change the past. I can go on now and try to do better though. I promise you one thing: you will never have any reason to doubt my truthfulness to you—ever, for as long as we live. When I first met you, I told you I wanted to be like you someday. Well, I feel that way again."

"How long will you be in town?" she asked wearily.

"About a week . . . if that's okay."

"Let's go then. I want to make sure the missionaries can come tonight." She started down the trail, and he followed.

"Jake, you're going to have to apologize to my mom and dad."

"I will. I'll do anything you ask."

"It's not going to be easy."

"I know that. If I do everything you ask me to, do you think there's a chance we could get married someday?" he asked.

She shook her head. "No, not really."

"Not even the remotest chance?"

"I don't think so. Sorry."

"Look, I'm talking . . . maybe one chance in ten million."

She shrugged her shoulders. "Well, maybe that, I suppose."

"All right! We're making progress! So, since we're

almost engaged, it'd probably be okay for us to kiss then, right?"

She shook her head. "It'll be a *long* time, if ever, before I'd feel comfortable with that."

"You think that's fair?"

"What are you talking about?"

"You let me kiss you when you thought we were cousins, for crying out loud. But now that we're thinking about getting married, you won't?"

"Give it a rest, Jake!"

He realized he'd made a big mistake. "Sorry."

She jogged down the trail to get away from him. He tried to keep up.

When they came to where the snow blocked the trail, he tossed a snowball at her and hit her in the back. She turned around and glared at him.

He approached Andrea, put his hands behind his back, and said, "Go ahead, I dare you." He opened his mouth wide.

It was such an inviting shot. She picked up some snow and tossed it in his face.

He smiled. And then she smiled. And the snowball fight was on.

They chased each other back and forth over the snow, laughing, giggling, threatening, pleading, demanding, until they were both out of breath and soaked.

He gathered up an armful of snow and heaved it straight up into the air. The sun's rays caught it and for an instant it was like individual droplets of sunlight were cascading around them.

It was a magical moment.

But that's all it was, a moment.

They started back down the trail. "You got any advice for me when I talk to your mom and dad?" he asked.

She smiled faintly. "Sure. Be prepared to duck."

9

Jake felt like he was walking into a bear's den with bacon strapped to his chest as Andrea led him into the house. "Mom, Dad," she called out.

"We're in the kitchen," her mom said.

"Is that okay?" she asked him privately. "You won't be too embarrassed sitting around the kitchen table with my folks?"

Jake, red-faced, nodded. "No, it'll be okay."

In the kitchen, Vernon stood up and shook Jake's hand. "Please sit down."

Marilyn tried to smile, but it was too much to ask. The effort froze on her face. "Hello, Jake."

They all sat at the kitchen table. "First of all," Jake said, "I want to apologize for the way I acted . . . before."

Marilyn pulled no punches. "You mean when you were telling one lie after another to my daughter?"

"But," Jake blurted out, "that was only after I realized that Andrea's no angel."

"Ouch," Andrea said softly, feeling more sorry for Jake than offended.

Marilyn, wild-eyed, stood up, ready to throw him out of the house. "I beg your pardon?"

"He meant *angel* literally, Mom," Andrea tried to explain.

"That's why we got along so well at first," Jake explained. "Because I thought I was dead."

"Are you saying that only a dead person could possibly get along with Andrea?" Marilyn raged.

Vernon put his hand on his wife's hand. "Marilyn, calm down."

Marilyn sat down. "How could you possibly think you were dead?"

"I hadn't eaten all day. And then this crazy conductor filled my head with stories of people who've had near-death experiences. When I left the train during the night, I ran into something and knocked myself out. I woke up a little later and saw a light approaching me, and then I passed out. The next morning when I woke up, there was Andrea, looking like an angel. She told me she was my cousin and that she'd been expecting me."

"You must have known she wasn't your cousin," Marilyn said.

"Not really. I'm not that close with my dad's side of the family."

"Why's that?"

"Because my dad walked out on us when I was twelve years old. We haven't seen him or anyone from his family since then."

Vernon put his hand on Jake's arm. "Jake, just go ahead with whatever you came here to say. And Marilyn, quit baiting the boy. He's doing the best he can."

Jake nodded. "Thank you, sir. I just want to say that I'm very sorry for what happened."

"You came back all this way just to apologize?" Marilyn asked.

"Yeah. And also because when I was in Seattle, I realized I'm in love with Andrea. In fact, I just asked her to marry me."

Vernon, who had been trying to be the calming influ-
ence, started coughing.

"Really?" Marilyn asked, her voice high and thin. She put
her hand to her forehead, then went to the cupboard. "Does
anyone else need any aspirin?"

"I do," Vernon said.

"Me too," Andrea echoed.

"Unless you have Tylenol," Jake said.

"This isn't a drugstore," Marilyn snapped.

"Aspirin's good," Jake said meekly.

Marilyn used a tray to bring four glasses, a bottle of
aspirin, and a pitcher of water to the table. "I guess I
could've put ice in the pitcher."

"No, this is fine," Vernon said.

They all downed their aspirin.

"Andrea, are you really considering marrying Jake?"
Vernon asked Andrea.

"No, of course not. I told him that right away."

"Oh, good," Marilyn said with a sigh of relief. "For a
minute there, I was really worried."

"Andrea gives me about a one-in-ten-million chance,"
Jake said. "You might think that'd discourage me, but it
doesn't."

"Why not?" Andrea asked.

Jake pulled a dollar bill from his wallet. "I fixed a math
teacher's car once who showed me this. What do you suppose the chances are that, of all the dollar bills in the country, I'd have the one with the serial number . . . " He read
the serial number. "What would be the odds of that? Maybe
one in ten million?" He waved the bill in Marilyn's face.
"Well, isn't that something? Here it is. Am I a lucky guy or
what?"

Marilyn wasn't impressed. "You say that, at first, you
thought you'd died. Okay, fine. Suppose I accept that. When
did you realize you weren't dead?"

"Right after I fell off the cliff."

"And that was when, a couple of hours later?" Marilyn asked.

"That's right."

Marilyn continued. "So, for the next two days, you tried to make us believe you were part of the family. Is that right?"

"I did it so I could spend more time with Andrea."

"Why did you want to spend time with her?" Marilyn asked. "What was really on your mind?"

"Mom!" Andrea complained.

"I just want to know why he kept lying to us, that's all," Marilyn answered. "He must have had a reason. For all we know, he was only looking for a summer conquest."

"That had nothing to do with it," Jake answered emphatically. "It was because I'd never met a girl like Andrea before. She's good and kind and at peace with herself. And she tries to help other people."

"How can we ever trust anything you say after what you've done?" Marilyn asked.

"Jake's agreed to take the missionary lessons," Andrea said.

Marilyn's frown softened a little.

"That's good," Vernon said.

"Excuse me. I've got a headache. I need to lie down," Marilyn said as she walked out of the room.

Andrea went to the cupboard. "Anyone want a cookie to go with your aspirin?" she asked.

Vernon shook his head. "I need to finish mowing the lawn." And then he left.

Jake, with his elbows on the table, cradled his head in his hands. "Oh, man, that was tough. I could really use a beer about now."

Andrea smiled and patted Jake on the back. "Poor Jake."

"What?"

"You've got so much to learn."

* * * * *

Elder Harbison from Nampa, Idaho, and Elder Steiner from San Clemente, California, came to give Jake the first discussion. They had dinner first and then went into the living room for the discussion. Andrea's mom and dad left to go grocery shopping.

Before his mission, during his freshman year at BYU, Elder Harbison had been on the BYU football team. He was six-foot-four and weighed two hundred and seventy-five pounds. Even though he was huge, he was easygoing and fun to be with.

Elder Steiner, thin and wiry, was very businesslike. He liked to keep things on target and had a habit of looking at his watch every few minutes.

Jake liked them both. They were easy to talk with and not at all as stuffy as he thought they'd be.

"What do you know about the Church?" Elder Harbison asked.

Jake wanted to impress them with what he'd picked up from Andrea. "Well, actually, I've been to the empty sea." He said it with the degree of seriousness the subject warranted.

"Really? When were you there?" Elder Steiner asked.

"I've been there many times."

"With family or friends?"

"Always alone. That's the way it is in the empty sea."

"What did you think about it?" Elder Harbison asked.

"I was always glad to get away."

"Tell me about it," Elder Harbison said, nodding his head.

Andrea suspected something was wrong. "Jake, have you ever been to Utah?"

"No."

"Then how could you visit the MTC?"

133

"You don't have to be in Utah to visit the empty sea. It's all around us."

The three of them looked at each other. Finally Andrea wrote something on a piece of paper and handed it to Jake. It read, "*Missionary Training Center or MTC.*"

After Jake read the paper, his face turned red. "Sorry."

"Don't worry about it," Elder Harbison said with a reassuring smile.

It was the smile that did it. Elder Harbison wasn't just saying it. He really meant it. As a result, Jake didn't worry about it.

After the discussion, Elder Steiner asked Jake to give the prayer. Jake said he didn't know how. Elder Steiner said he'd teach him. A few minutes later they knelt down while Jake self-consciously said the prayer. He felt it wasn't very good, but everyone seemed happy he'd done it.

Jake asked if they could teach him every day until he left. They said they could.

He walked with them out to their car. He noticed one of the windshield wipers was tied down with string. When he asked about it, they said it had come loose and didn't work. They had tied it down so it wouldn't flap back and forth when they went fast.

Things like that bothered Jake.

* * * * *

The discussion was over at seven-thirty. Andrea asked Jake if he'd like to go canoeing on the lake by Grampa's cabin.

It was a new experience for him, and he nearly tipped them over, just getting into the canoe. But Andrea coached him, and they were soon gliding across the water. She sat in the back to steer while he took the front.

Andrea had brought snacks.

"Want a carrot stick?" she asked

"What for? My mom isn't here. I can eat anything I want."

"Carrots are good for you."

"Forget what I said about a mom not being here."

They moved almost silently across the lake. For a long time they didn't talk. They got into a rhythm of paddling and then gliding effortlessly across the water. They found a small cove and, using a flashlight, took turns reading from the Book of Mormon.

"What do you think about what we just read?" she asked an hour later as they headed back.

"It's okay."

"Just okay?"

"I don't know. It's all so new. I mean, what do you want me to say?"

"I know it's true."

"What do you mean, you *know* it's true?" he asked.

"I mean I know it's true. It's more than just a belief with me." She paused. "And it can be that way for you, if you want it to be."

"Okay, what would I have to do?"

She read from Moroni, chapter ten, verses four and five.

"I've read that before."

"When?"

"When I was here before."

"When did you have a chance to read from the Book of Mormon?"

Jake stuck with his recent decision to always tell the truth. "It was just before the funeral. While you were taking a shower, I went in your room to look for the cashier's check."

After a long silence, she asked, "You were in my room?"

"Just for a few minutes."

"My gosh, Jake, how many more of these little surprises have you got for me?"

"That's the last one. Anyway, there was a book on your

desk. I looked through it, hoping to find my check. I read one of the underlined parts. It was what you just read."

Andrea shook her head. "I can't believe you were in my room. Did you look anywhere else besides my Book of Mormon?"

"Well, in your desk drawer."

"You went through my things?"

"Just the desk drawer, okay?"

"Why just the desk drawer?"

"Because you turned off the water in the shower and, also, because your mom came in the house."

"What did you do?"

"Went downstairs. Your mom saw me and asked me what I was doing upstairs."

"What did you say?"

"I told her I'd gone up there to ask you to hurry up."

"So, once again, Jake serves up another big, fat lie!"

Jake cleared his throat. "I guess you could say that."

"Of course I can say it! Because it's the truth. I can't believe you were in my room going through my things!"

"I didn't go through your clothes drawers if that's what you're worried about."

"I'm not sure I believe that, but even if it's true, the only reason you didn't go through everything is because you didn't have enough time. Right?"

He cleared his throat. "That's probably true."

"I know this may be news to you, but if you're going to be a member of the Church, you can't go ransacking through other people's things."

"You don't have to tell me that, okay?" he snapped.

"Well, somebody has to. Do you even know the difference between lying and telling the truth?"

Jake was embarrassed. Getting caught at every turn was no fun. In his frustration, he made the mistake of saying a couple of swear words.

"Don't you ever talk like that around me again!"

"Sorry, it just slipped out."

"I don't understand why you even came back here."

"Because I love you. Because I want to marry you."

"I will never, ever marry someone I don't respect."

"Then I'll do everything I can to gain your respect."

There was a long pause and then she said softly, "It's too late for that, Jake."

"I can't accept that," he said.

They reached shore and managed to beach the canoe without tipping over. Then, together, they carried it up the hill and stowed it under the cabin.

As they walked in the dark toward Andrea's home, she was the first to speak. "I'm glad you're taking the missionary lessons, and I don't want to discourage you from that. Just don't expect me to marry you as a reward for joining the Church. That's not the way it works."

They walked the rest of the way home in silence. He didn't even hold her hand.

At the door, she said, "Goodnight."

"Is it?" he asked, and then left.

Back at the cabin, Jake sat in the rocking chair and looked at the stars. *Andrea's right,* he thought. *I have no business being here. I should just clear out tonight. No need to say good-bye. Just go. Start hitchhiking. See how far I can get before morning. Who was I trying to fool anyway? No matter how hard I try, it'll never be good enough for Andrea. So why even try?*

He went inside and packed his things. On his way out, he decided to leave a note. He found a notepad in the desk drawer.

Dear Andrea. He crumpled the paper up and threw it in the waste paper basket. He was mad at her and was not about to call her *dear.*

137

Andrea,

I've had it with you, your family, and your religion.

He crumpled it up. *Too bitter,* he thought.

He tried again.

Andrea,

Actually I prefer being in the empty sea. Good-bye.

Jake.

He left the note on the table, picked up his gym bag, and walked out the door.

Half an hour later he was on the highway hitchhiking. None of the few cars that passed by stopped.

He was still there at midnight. He was tired so he went back to the cabin. His plan was to get a few hours sleep and take the morning train back to Seattle.

As he sat down on the edge of the bed to take off his shoes, he noticed Grampa's copy of the Book of Mormon.

Read it, he thought.

I'm too tired, he answered back.

Once again the thought came into his mind. *Read it.*

No, I've given that all up. It's not for me.

He turned out the light.

Just skim it then, the thought persisted.

He punched up the pillow to make it more fluffy. *No, I'm tired. I'm going to sleep now.*

No, you're not. He could hear water dripping from the bathroom faucet. Each drop seemed like the beat of a drum.

As he got up out of bed to turn off the faucet, he used every swear word he'd ever heard, just to make it obvious to whatever voice was trying to get him to read that he wasn't exactly a good candidate.

He tried to stop the water from dripping, but, somehow, in tightening it, he made it worse. He swore at the faucet, returned to bed, and wrapped the pillow over his head to shut out the noise.

It didn't do any good.

Maybe God's trying to tell me something, he thought.

Jake went outside on the porch and looked heavenward. "Just leave me alone. I'm not worth it. Can't you see that? I'll never change. You know me. So why do you keep bothering me?"

Suddenly a thought, not from him, came clearly and calmly into his mind. *Because* I know you.

Jake went inside, put on his slacks, sat down, and began skimming the Book of Mormon. He was looking for something. The only problem was he didn't know what.

He found it in the gray light of dawn. It was in Mosiah, chapter 27, where Alma the younger, almost as if he were talking to Jake, gave this comforting message.

I have repented of my sins, and have been redeemed of the Lord; behold I am born of the Spirit . . . the Lord in mercy hath seen fit to snatch me out of an everlasting burning, and I am born of God. My soul hath been redeemed from the gall of bitterness and bonds of iniquity. I was in the darkest abyss; but now I behold the marvelous light of God. My soul was racked with eternal torment; but I am snatched, and my soul is pained no more.

Jake, finally, had his answer. There was hope for him.

* * * * *

He was still sleeping when he heard a knock on the door. He knew it wasn't Andrea because she was lifeguarding at the city pool. He put on a pair of slacks and a shirt and went to the door.

It was the elders.

"Did you forget about us coming?" Elder Harbison asked.

"No, sorry, I must have slept in. I can be ready in a minute. C'mon in."

Jake threw some water on his face, dried off, and then came out of the bathroom into the kitchen of the cabin.

"Could we do the lesson on the porch?" Jake suggested. "It's such a nice day."

When they were finished, Elder Harbison told him it was the easiest discussion he'd ever given. Jake answered all the questions and made all the commitments.

"Well, then, that's it," Elder Harbison said.

"Can you give me another discussion now?"

"We'd like to," Elder Steiner said, "but we have a zone conference."

"What's that?"

"All the missionaries working around here get together for training," Elder Harbison said. "You want to come along?"

Elder Steiner shook his head. "I don't know, Elder . . ."

"What would I do?"

"Well, you could listen in," Elder Harbison said.

"Could I work on your cars?" Jake asked.

"Sure, why not?" Elder Harbison said enthusiastically.

"Elder Harbison, I'm not sure . . ." Elder Steiner began.

"I'd like that," Jake said. "I don't have anything else to do today anyway."

* * * * *

Jake wasn't sure why he felt so good working on the missionary cars, but he did. Replacing a broken rearview mirror for the sisters' car and fixing the wipers of Elder Harbison and Elder Steiner's car was easy. But he felt useful. It was kind of like a gift. That was it. It was his offering to the Lord.

After a couple of hours the missionaries took a break, and Elder Harbison and Elder Steiner came out of the chapel to the parking lot to see how he was doing. By that time he was just finishing up fixing a car window that had been stuck half-open.

"Boy, you're doing a great job!" Elder Harbison said.

"You're going to have some happy people when they see what you've done."

"Thanks. I enjoyed doing it."

"You know, you could do this on your mission," Elder Harbison said. "You'd be great at it too."

"Really?"

"Absolutely. Look, the reason we came out is because we're having testimonies now. C'mon in and see what that's like."

Jake sat with Elder Harbison and Elder Steiner. It was an amazing experience to listen to guys his age talk about their feelings about the work they were doing as missionaries. Even though some of them became emotional while they were talking, they were all obviously happy doing what they were doing. It didn't seem so strange when the sister missionaries expressed love for each other, but it made Jake uncomfortable when any of the elders said he loved his companion. Even Elder Harbison, as big and tough-looking as he appeared, told Elder Steiner that he loved him.

After the meeting, Elder Harbison put his arm around Jake's shoulder and said, "You'd be a good missionary, Jake."

* * * * *

That night Jake phoned his mom. "Mom, I'm going to do a movie for Dwight Stone. He wants me to be the next James Dean. We'll be shooting the movie in Argentina. Oh, also, I'm studying to be a Mormon."

There was a long pause. "Who are you, and what have you done with my son?"

"It's true, Mom."

"Are you happy? That's the important thing."

"I am, Mom. Really happy."

"Is Glacier Gal talking to you now?"

"She is. I asked her to marry me."

141

"What did she say?"

"She says my chances are about ten million to one."

"Sounds like she's head over heels in love with you. When's the big day?"

"Probably never, but the soonest it could be is about a year away."

"She can't get a hair appointment any sooner?"

"She wants to get married in a Mormon temple."

"Why's that?"

"If you get married in the temple, it's forever, even after you die."

"A marriage that never ends?" She sighed. "So tell me, people actually want this?"

"They do, Mom. They call it eternal marriage."

"Most women I know feel like their marriage has already lasted an eternity. By the way, have they said if there's Valium in Heaven?"

"They haven't said one way or the other."

"If they don't have it, I'm not going." She paused. "So, are you really thinking of becoming a Mormon?" she asked.

"I am, Mom."

"They're the ones with the free TV offers, right? How do they get by giving away so much stuff?"

"That's just the way they are."

"Well, if you're happy, that's the most important thing."

"I'm going back to Seattle on Tuesday. I'll call you when I get there."

"Natasha still asks about you. You could still have her, if you act now, but if you wait around much longer, she'll probably marry Carl."

"I'm glad for her, Mom."

"Okay, this is my last offer: Natasha turns Mormon, moves to Montana, and starts a goat ranch. Interested?"

"I've pretty much got my eye on Andrea right now."

His mom sighed. "It was worth a shot," she said.

10

The next morning the elders gave Jake another discussion. Each one seemed almost too easy. The concepts made sense. In many instances they were things Jake had believed all along: that God was his Father in Heaven, that God was a person, that just as there had been prophets long ago, there could be prophets today.

What was hard about the discussions was that, with each one, Jake made commitments about how he'd live the rest of his life. Those commitments were starting to pile up. It was one thing to say you believed something. It was quite another to say you'd change your lifestyle—completely.

After the discussion that day, Jake began to worry if he'd be able to live the way he'd said he would. He became discouraged. It seemed as though they were asking too much. It was like they were chipping away at who he was, and that he was giving up more and more of himself with each discussion.

In the afternoon he went to the swimming pool to be with Andrea while she worked. It was a bright, sunny day, and the sun highlighted the copper tones in her hair. She wore a modest one-piece swimming suit with a baggy T-shirt so all that was exposed were her legs.

The way she was with kids enchanted him. While she

was lifeguarding, even though she never took her eyes off the swimmers, she carried on a conversation with two or three of them at a time. She seemed to be delighted by every boy or girl.

When he first walked into the pool wearing the swimming suit he'd just bought, a little of the old Jake surfaced. He was privately glad Andrea would get to see him in a swimming suit. For so long his body had been one of the best things about him. It was hard for him to give that up.

He hoped it'd get warm enough so Andrea would take her T-shirt off. But then he felt guilty for thinking that because, earlier that day, he'd committed to living the law of chastity. The idea of checking Andrea out didn't seem to fit in with living a chaste life.

Jake didn't like this infighting with himself. It never used to happen, but now that he was learning about the Church, he could see that the inner conflicts would be a part of his life until he threw out some of his old thought patterns.

He walked over and said hello to Andrea, but he almost had to stand in line because of the boys and girls who were jockeying for position to be near her.

Wearing a big grin, he stood on tiptoe and said over the top of the crowd, "I'm going swimming now, but I'm not very good, so you may have to rescue me."

She smiled back, but it somehow depressed him. It was the same smile she gave everyone. *She's keeping her distance because she doesn't trust me anymore,* he thought.

"Do you have any sunscreen?" she asked. "I've got some you can use."

He shrugged his shoulders. "Sure. Thanks."

Jake stood next to her lifeguard chair and rubbed on sunscreen. The kids standing around her chair were jabbering at her, and she seemed to be taking a genuine interest in what they were saying.

When he finished with the sunscreen, Jake reached up to hand her the tube. "I had another lesson this morning."

"How'd it go?"

"Good."

"I'm glad. I think it's better for me not to be there when you have the discussions. I mean, this is between you and the missionaries, right?"

"Yeah, I guess so."

Jake got into the pool. It was too crowded with screaming, laughing kids to do much swimming, so after treading water for a time, he got out and dried himself off, sat down on his towel, and watched Andrea work her magic with the children.

* * * * *

Later that afternoon Jake returned to Andrea's home. Marilyn was in the backyard working in the garden.

"Need any help?" he asked.

"Sure, that'd be nice. I've neglected it lately, what with the funeral and all. You could start weeding over there. Yank out everything that doesn't look like a tomato plant."

"This?" he asked

"No, that's a tomato plant. That's what we're trying to keep."

"Oh, yeah, sure. Like this, for instance, right?"

"That's right."

"I got it," he said, pulling out a weed.

"Did you have a nice time swimming?" Marilyn asked.

"Yeah, I did. Andrea is really good with kids. She's the most amazing girl I've ever met."

Marilyn looked over at Jake and smiled. "I feel the same way."

"I just want you to know that if Andrea and I do end up getting married, I'll always be good to her."

"I'm glad to hear that."

They returned to their work. A few minutes later, Marilyn asked, "If you and Andrea were to get married, how would you support a family?"

"Well, if this movie works out, I should do pretty well being an actor."

"What if it doesn't?"

"I don't know. Maybe come back here and fix cars."

"That'd be nice for us because it'd give us a chance to spoil our grandchildren. I take it you're not interested in going to college. Is that right?"

"I've just never thought about it. I wasn't a very good student in high school. Too many other things going on."

"I'm sure you could do very well in college, if you put your mind to it."

"Could be. I'll think about it."

They worked in silence for a few minutes.

"Do you always have a garden?" Jake asked.

"Every year," Marilyn answered. "I think it's because we have such hard winters. Some years from October to April, there's snow on the ground. It's as if everything has died, and you begin to wonder if the cold and the snow will ever end. In February, the seed and bulb catalogs come. I always buy too much. And then the snow melts, and the grass turns green, and then one morning I spot a tulip starting to come out of the ground, and suddenly the world is a wonderful place. Around here, spring brings hope and joy."

Jake smiled. "In Chicago, you know it's spring when they start tearing up the roads. Of course, then you have delays and detours. I like your celebration of spring better."

When Jake finished weeding the tomatoes, Marilyn showed him how to apply tomato dust to discourage bugs from attacking the leaves.

She asked about his family. He told her about his mother

146

and how hard she had had to work when his dad walked out.

As the afternoon wore on, and they each began to open up, Jake felt, once again, a part of the family.

"I think we've accomplished a great deal this afternoon," Marilyn said as they carried their tools back to the garage.

"I agree," Jake said with a smile.

* * * * *

The next day, while Andrea was working, Vernon asked Jake if he'd like to do some fishing. He readily agreed.

They fished from a boat at McDonald Lake, not far from town. They had been fishing in silence when Jake said, "How do you think things are going for me as far as Andrea is concerned?"

"A little better, I'd say."

"Really?"

"Sure. You're pretty much doing what she'd like you to do. That always makes it easy." Vernon paused. "There's just one thing, though, you might want to think about."

"What's that?"

"I'm not sure this will make much sense to you, or if I can even explain it."

Jake had brought along a bag of corn chips. He took some and handed the bag to Vernon. Vernon grabbed a handful, then said, "Think about this. Let's say five years have passed, and you and Andrea are married. We'll consider two scenarios. The first is this. She reminds you it's near the end of the month, and that you ought to do your home teaching. So you go home teaching. Every night, when it's time for your kids to go to bed, she tells you that you should have family prayer, so you call on her to give the prayer. Every couple of months she says she thinks you two ought to go to the temple. So you do. She keeps after you to do one thing after another. And you do. Okay, that's the first scenario."

"That doesn't sound too bad," Jake said.

"No, it isn't, not really. But here's the other scenario. She doesn't need to remind you to do the things you're supposed to do. You do them because you have the light of the gospel in your own life. Which of the two do you think Andrea would prefer?"

"The second."

Vernon nodded. "That's right. A woman doesn't want to have to keep after her husband to do what's right. She wants him to take the lead. But I'm afraid you're in a pattern of doing what she wants. And, if that continues, then in five years she's going to be wishing you were stronger."

"How do I get to be stronger?"

Vernon shook his head. "I don't know what to tell you. I know how some young men your age get that inner strength."

"How?"

"They serve two-year missions. When they come back from that experience, most of them are rock-solid in their commitment to live the gospel. They make better husbands, fathers, and even employees."

Grabbing another handful of chips, Jake nodded and then changed the subject. Going on a mission was out of the question. What he wanted to do was marry Andrea as soon as he could. He was not going to worry about how disillusioned Andrea might be in five or ten years.

"Andrea has a friend named Ben who's serving a mission, right?" Jake asked.

"That's right. They were friends all through high school. They were the only members of the Church in their class."

"I suppose you always pictured Andrea marrying him."

"Not so much him as someone like him. The Church is very important in Ben's life."

148

"I'm glad she had someone like that when she was growing up."

"Are you jealous of him?"

"I guess I am. I'd like to marry Andrea before he gets back from his mission."

Vernon laughed. "Well, you're thinking like a Mormon already. From what Andrea says, that's the way things work at Ricks."

Vernon hooked into a fish. Jake grabbed a net as Vernon reeled in, then dipped the net into the water and lifted a three-pound trout into the boat. Vernon removed the hook, held it up by the gills to show it off, then lowered it back into the water. He held it there until it recovered enough to dart away.

"Good job," Jake said.

"Thanks. It's your turn now," Vernon said.

"I'm ready."

Out of the corner of his eye, Jake studied Vernon. A little overweight, with thin islands of hair on an otherwise bald head, Andrea's dad was a man who might easily be overlooked in a crowd. But hanging on a bulletin board in the Warner's kitchen was a newspaper article about Vernon in his role as principal of the local elementary school. At the beginning of school the previous fall, he had promised the students that if they would read 10,000 books during the school year, he'd dive into a 200-gallon batch of macaroni and cheese.

What student could resist that? They had met the challenge.

In the article, there was a picture showing Vernon in a Hawaii flowered shirt and Bermuda shorts, wearing swimming goggles, standing above a large black trash container, surrounded by all the students and the teachers in the school.

When Jake had first read the article and seen the picture,

he felt embarrassed for Vernon because he'd made such a fool of himself. But when he studied the picture and focused on the students standing around with big grins on their faces, he realized the whole thing was about the love of a man for the children he was given each year. All Vernon had wanted to do was to change their lives.

He must love those kids very much to do something like that, Jake thought.

"I read the article about you jumping in the macaroni and cheese," Jake said. "What are you going to do next year?"

"I don't know. You got any ideas?"

"No, not really. I just think it's great you do that to get everybody reading."

"It's a lot of fun. All through the year kids run up to me and say, 'I read five books over the weekend!' And I get this worried look and say, 'Don't read so much! Watch more TV.' And they laugh and tell me they're not going to do it, that they're going to keep reading. And I tell 'em, 'Oh, no! I can see I'm in big trouble!'"

"I admire you for doing that."

"It works. You ever think about teaching?"

"No, not me. I wasn't that good in school."

"It doesn't matter. You can do anything you want, once you make up your mind to do it."

He smiled. "Well, I hope so. That's why I'm here."

"Because you want to marry Andrea?"

"Right. Do you have any advice for me, you know, about Andrea?"

"Don't join the Church just because of her. It won't do either one of you any good. You need to keep those two things separate. First, decide if the Church is true and if you're willing to make it a part of your life. Then worry about what's going to happen between you and Andrea. Don't mix the two together."

150

"That's hard to do," Jake said.

"I know it is, but I think you need to ask yourself, 'What if I join the Church and Andrea ends up marrying someone else? Will I still live the way the Church teaches? Do I really believe this, or am I just doing it for Andrea's sake?'"

"I'll keep that in mind."

"If it's any consolation, no matter what happens between you two, anytime you show up around here, I'd be honored to have you as a fishing partner."

Jake smiled. "Thanks. I appreciate that. You've been really good to me."

"That's because I see a lot of good in you."

Jake turned away because he felt a rush of emotion, and he didn't want Vernon to know about it. He felt deprived, not having had a dad around when he was growing up, somebody he could talk to man-to-man, someone older who'd lived enough of life to have some perspective.

He wanted to say something to Vernon, but he didn't know how. Finally, right after Vernon said he thought it was time they head back to shore, Jake blurted out, "One of the nice things about marrying Andrea would be that I'd get to call you 'Dad.'"

Vernon nodded, blinked, then said, "I guess we'll just have to see how it all works out." After a moment, he added, "But I will tell you this—I'd like that too."

* * * * *

On Sunday Jake went to church with Andrea and her folks. The building was not very impressive compared to the churches he'd seen back home in Chicago.

A large lumber-jack type of guy, with no neck but a big smile, came up to meet Jake. He shook Jake's hand and welcomed him to church. After they sat down in the chapel, Andrea said, "That man is our branch president."

151

The word *branch* threw Jake off. "He trims branches for a living?"

"No. He's like the minister for our group. Except he doesn't get paid, and he has a regular job. Those two men sitting next to him are his counselors."

"He's getting counseling?" Jake asked.

"No, they're his helpers."

"Oh."

She leaned over and whispered. "Nobody in the Church gets paid for the work they do in the Church. They're all volunteers."

"Listening to that woman play the organ, I can believe it," Jake said.

"Shush," Andrea said, jabbing him gently in the ribs.

The lumberjack-in-a-suit got up to speak. "We'd like to welcome you to sacrament meeting . . . "

It was a strange thing about that meeting. On the one hand, it was obvious these people weren't professionals, such as Jake had seen in the churches he'd gone to in Chicago. If anything, these people all seemed a little apologetic about everything they did. And yet there was undeniable power somewhere. He could sense it. It was hard to explain what he felt, but he did feel something—something warm and comfortable that made it feel as though he had come home.

What added to that was how friendly everyone was. Almost everyone greeted him and made him feel welcome. They even thanked him for coming as they introduced themselves.

One of them said, "I'm so glad you're investigating the Church."

When she left, he turned to Andrea. "Am I investigating the Church?"

"It just means you're taking the missionary lessons."

"Chief Investigator Jake. I like the sound of that."

"Let's go to Sunday School class."

Jake learned that he got his very own Sunday School class, conducted just for him. Andrea called it the Gospel Essentials class.

"Does that mean there's a class called the Gospel Non-essentials?"

"Shush," she said.

Once again, the two opposing thoughts came to Jake's mind: one, *These people aren't very polished,* and two, *So why do I feel so good being with them?*

After Sunday School class was over, Jake went with Elder Harbison and Elder Steiner to what they called priesthood meeting. The teacher gave him a manual. He glanced through it during the lesson. Some of it he couldn't understand, but from what he could understand, it looked as though the men spent a lot of time learning to be better husbands and fathers. *That can't be a bad thing,* he thought.

During part of the lesson Jake closed his eyes. What he was hearing didn't seem that great—men just talking about what they believed, not a bit flashy. And yet he felt much more than the words should have made him feel, almost at times filling him with hope.

Later that Sunday, in a missionary discussion, Jake agreed to be baptized the next day. On Tuesday he would leave for Seattle.

* * * * *

That night Jake couldn't sleep. Someone inside his mind was talking to him. *Are you out of your mind? The only reason you're doing this is for Andrea. But you're leaving tomorrow. And then what will you do? Are you saying you're not going to want to have a beer once in a while if someone offers it to you? You think you're better than everybody else? Well, you're not.*

Like some perverse parade celebrating evil, all the things he'd done wrong in his life flooded into his mind. *It's too late for you. Give it up.*

No, he answered back, *I just need to talk to someone.*

A few minutes later he stood at Andrea's front door. He looked at his watch. It was one-fifteen in the morning. He knocked softly but nobody answered. *If I ring the bell, I'm going to wake up everyone, including Andrea,* he thought. He didn't want to talk to Andrea.

He tried the door. It was open. He stepped inside and closed the door behind him. *They really should lock the door at night,* he thought.

He made his way to Vernon and Marilyn's bedroom. The door was shut. He knocked softly. There was no answer. He knocked again. Still no answer.

He opened the door just a crack. "Excuse me," he said softly.

Still no answer. He walked over to the bed. "I hate to bother you both this time of night, but . . . "

Marilyn woke up and saw a stranger standing over her muttering something. She gasped.

"Don't worry. It's just me," Jake said.

"Good grief, Jake, you scared me to death. How did you get in?"

"I knocked first but nobody answered, and the door was unlocked, so I . . . "

"Is there something wrong?" she asked.

"Not really. Vernon?" Jake called.

"Yes," Vernon answered faintly.

"I was wondering if I could talk to you."

"Can't this wait until morning?" Marilyn asked.

"Well, I guess it could, but, the truth is, I'm having kind of a bad night."

"It's okay," Vernon assured his wife as he got out of bed.

154

Vernon put on a robe and slippers. Jake followed him as he padded out to the kitchen.

"Would you like anything to eat?" Vernon asked.

"No, thanks."

They sat down. "You say you're having a bad night? What seems to be the trouble?"

"Basically, I'd say my problem is . . . " Jake felt foolish. *It was a mistake to have even come here. He doesn't want to hear this.* The grandfather clock in the living room did one bong for one-thirty. Jake wiped his brow. "My problem is . . . my past."

Vernon nodded. "I see."

"I've made some mistakes."

"It happens."

Jake couldn't look him in the eye. "This is really embarrassing. You probably think that when I say I've made some mistakes that I mean I got a traffic ticket or I forgot to return a book to the library." Jake turned away. He didn't want Vernon to see his tears. "But that's not what I mean. I'm not talking about little mistakes. I'm talking about more serious things."

"I understand."

"I've been going over them in my mind tonight. That's why I haven't been able to sleep."

"You were interviewed for baptism, weren't you?"

"Yes, sir."

"Were you honest in that interview?" Vernon asked.

"Yes, sir. But most of the interview had to do with if I'm willing to live the commandments from now on. It wasn't about the past. My past. My mistakes." He shook his head. "I don't know why I keep calling them mistakes." He took a deep breath. "They weren't mistakes. They were sins. I didn't know it at the time, but now I do. So I'm wondering if maybe I should really be a part of your church."

155

Vernon excused himself. In a minute he came back with his scriptures.

"If Elder Harbison feels you are ready to be baptized, I trust his judgment." He paused. "But there is one thing about what you're saying that troubles me."

"What?"

"You don't seem to understand why it's possible for us to have hope." He turned to a passage in the Book of Mormon. "Read verses 13 through 15."

Jake began to read.

And Aaron did expound unto him the scriptures from the creation of Adam, laying the fall of man before him, and their carnal state and also the plan of redemption, which was prepared from the foundation of the world, through Christ, for all whosoever would believe on his name.

And since man had fallen he could not merit anything of himself; but the sufferings and death of Christ atone for their sins, through faith and repentance, and so forth; and that he breaketh the bands of death, that the grave shall have no victory, and that the sting of death should be swallowed up in the hopes of glory; and Aaron did expound all these things unto the king.

And it came to pass that after Aaron had expounded these things unto him, the king said: What shall I do that I may have this eternal life of which thou has spoken? Yea, what shall I do that I may be born of God, having this wicked spirit rooted out of my breast, and receive his Spirit, that I may be filled with joy, that I may not be cast off at the last day? Behold, said he, I will give up all that I possess, yea, I will forsake my kingdom, that I may receive this great joy.

"Is being filled with joy something you want in your life?" Vernon asked.

"Yes, sir, I do."

"Then you may be interested in the king's prayer. Please read verse 18."

Jake began to read.

O God, Aaron hath told me that there is a God; and if there is a God, and if thou art God, wilt thou make thyself known unto me, and I will give away all my sins to know thee, and that I may be raised from the dead, and be saved at the last day.

Vernon looked Jake in the eye. "I guess the question is, are you willing to give away your sins? What that means is, are you willing to never return to them?"

Jake swallowed. It wouldn't be easy, but that is what he wanted. "I am willing to do that."

"Then I'd say you are ready. Getting baptized isn't just about joining a church. It's a two-way promise between you and Father in Heaven. It's receiving forgiveness for sins because of the atonement of Jesus Christ. We owe everything to the Savior for the great gift he gave us."

Vernon turned to another scripture, this one in the Doctrine and Covenants, and read it out loud.

Remember the worth of souls is great in the sight of God; For, behold, the Lord your Redeemer suffered death in the flesh; wherefore he suffered the pain of all men, that all men might repent and come unto him. And he hath risen again from the dead, that he might bring all men unto him, on conditions of repentance. And how great is his joy in the soul that repenteth!

They talked and read and talked some more, until it was two-thirty in the morning.

Jake finally stood up. "I'd better let you get some sleep. Thank you very much. I really appreciate you taking the time. I feel a lot better now. I'm definitely going to get baptized tomorrow."

"I'm glad to hear that." Vernon put his arm on Jake's back and patted it twice. "I never did have a son, you know." They started for the front door.

Jake smiled. "Where do I sign up?"

Vernon smiled. "I'll check with my lawyer in the morning and get the forms made up."

"The only problem is, Andrea and I would be relatives again. That's not the way I want to be a part of Andrea's family."

"We'll just make it unofficial then," Vernon said, putting his arms around Jake and pulling him close. "I'm very pleased with the changes I see you making in your life."

Jake held on long after Vernon might have wanted to break free. When they did pull apart, Jake felt embarrassed at the tears shining in his eyes. He felt as though he should give some kind of explanation. "My dad walked out a long time ago, so I guess in a way, well, . . . I hope you understand."

"I'm pleased you'd think of me that way."

The world seemed a much safer place as Jake walked back to the cabin that night.

Before he went to bed, he read once again what Vernon had read from the Doctrine and Covenants. But this time he read the next few verses.

Wherefore, you are called to cry repentance unto this people. And if it so be that you should labor all your days crying repentance unto this people, and bring, save it be one soul unto me, how great shall be your joy with him in the kingdom of my Father!

Jake was still thinking about that when he finally fell asleep.

* * * * *

Jake was baptized late Monday afternoon by Elder Harbison. Vernon confirmed him a member of the Church. Andrea sang what was becoming their theme song, "Amazing Grace."

After the service, the branch president interviewed Jake

about receiving the priesthood. Because Jake was leaving the next day, it was decided to perform the ordinance a few minutes later.

After his interview, he went to get Andrea. "They're going to make me a priest. Want to be there?"

"Of course I do."

"My mom always wanted me to be a priest."

Andrea smiled.

"It's quite a bit the same, you know, with celibacy and everything, except with the Mormons, there's no Bingo," he said.

She suppressed a grin. "I can see some things haven't changed."

"No, you're wrong. Everything has changed. For the first time in my life, I have something to hold onto."

"I know. I can see it in your eyes."

Once Andrea and her folks were in the office, Jake asked Vernon to ordain him a priest.

Vernon gave him a good blessing. Jake felt so much different than he'd ever felt before. He felt clean and whole and accepted by Father in Heaven, and that all his past sins had been washed away. It was an amazing feeling.

The Warners invited the missionaries to join them, and the little group went home for supper. For the next few hours, Jake felt cradled in love and approval.

At one point, Andrea's mom asked him to go in the backyard with her to help her pick some lettuce for sandwiches.

"Well, Jake, you've come a long way," she said.

"Yes, Ma'am."

"I think I owe you an apology," she said.

"How come?"

"I wasn't very supportive when you showed up to announce you'd just proposed to Andrea. I hope you understand. I just want the best for Andrea."

"I understand."

"Vernon says that, as far as I'm concerned, no boy will ever be good enough for her."

"That's probably true."

"I just want you to know that . . . I look at you with much greater respect than I ever thought possible."

"Thank you. I appreciate that."

She stood up. "I think that's enough lettuce for now."

They went back inside.

After they finished eating, while they were still at the kitchen table, Marilyn brought out a gift-wrapped package. "Jake, this is for you," she said.

He opened it and found out it was the Book of Mormon, the one Jake had been reading at the cabin.

"This was Grampa's book," Marilyn said. "I know you've been reading it, and . . . well, I know he'd want you to have it."

On nearly every page were notes and underlined passages put there by Grampa. "This is the best gift I've ever received," he said, his voice choked with emotion. "I'll take good care of it."

"I know you will." She came over and gave him a hug. Considering how much against him she'd been, it was one of the best parts of the day for Jake.

At nine-thirty Elder Steiner looked at his watch then glanced at Elder Harbison, who nodded and said, "We'd better be going."

Jake realized this might be the last time he would see them. "I'll walk you guys out to the car."

It was awkward at the car. "Well, thanks for everything," Jake stammered.

Elder Harbison threw his arms around him and hugged him. "I love you, Jake," he said.

Jake felt awkward. *Guys don't say this,* he thought. He backed away.

"I owe you guys a lot," he managed to say.

"We enjoyed teaching you," Elder Steiner said, shaking Jake's hand.

They got in the car. Jake watched them leave, then said quietly, "I love you guys too. Thanks for giving me a life."

He went back inside. Andrea's parents went to bed, but Jake and Andrea sat at the kitchen table and talked.

"I'm so proud of you for being baptized," she said as she brought them a plate of cookies.

"Thanks for being such a good example," he said.

"I didn't do anything. What will you do after you finish the movie?"

"I'm not sure. Your mom suggested I think about going to college. I wonder if I could get into Ricks?"

Andrea smiled. "You think you could make a really good stuffed bear?"

"I think so."

"Well, Rick doesn't let in just anybody. But if you can do a bear, I think you're in."

"Great." He paused. "So, are there a lot of girls like you at Ricks?"

"Oh, sure, lots of 'em."

"Maybe you could introduce me to some of them."

Her smile faded. "I guess I could."

"What about the girls in your apartment?" he asked.

"You wouldn't like them," she said, much too quickly.

"How can you be so sure?"

"Last spring, I caught one of 'em drinking my milk—from the carton."

"That's bad?"

"Are you kidding! That's as bad as it gets. You don't want to have anything to do with a girl like that."

"Well, what about one of the others?" he asked.

"One of them hums while she eats her cereal in the morning. So you can pretty much forget about her."

"Other than that, she's a nice girl, though, right?"

"I suppose. Except she's memorized dialogue from past episodes of *The Simpsons*. Being with her is like watching reruns twenty-four hours a day."

"Who else you got?"

"Jamie. But she's too fussy about being tidy. One time I moved all the pictures on her desk half an inch. She noticed. So she's out."

"There must be somebody at Ricks you could line me up with."

"What's wrong with me?" she blurted out.

"You?" he teased.

"Oh, just forget about it, okay? Excuse me, I need to take a walk."

He ran after her out the door and down the street. "Why do you always run away when you get mad?"

"I'm not running away. I'm taking a walk."

"It looks to me like you're running away. You know what? I'd love to hear what your roommates say about you."

They ended up sitting on a bench in front of the train station.

"What's wrong?" he asked.

"I don't know." She bit her lip. "I guess maybe I like you more than I thought I did."

"Oh, really?" He broke into a big grin. "How come?" he asked.

"I don't know. It's a little confusing. You're not the man of my dreams, that's for sure."

"Thanks a lot."

"It's nothing personal."

"I know. It never is between us." He patted her on the back. "Well, that's it then. That leaves us as friends. And of course, that's what you want. So that's it. Tell me some more about your roommates."

"Which one?"

"Hmmm. It's a tough choice. How about the hummer?" he said.

"Leave her out of this, okay?" she snapped. "Let me finish what I was saying. You're not the man of my dreams now, but you might be someday. I mean, look at how much you've changed in just a few days."

"Oh, I get it. With you it's like playing the stock market. You buy low and wait for the price to go up."

"I'm sorry. That sounds so cold and heartless, doesn't it?" Andrea said.

"No, not at all. You're taking a big chance when you marry a guy. Most of the guys I've known in my life, I'd never marry. I mean, if I was a girl. Guys are kind of like a new car assembled at a factory where everyone's out on strike, put together by nonunion labor. Guys need a lot of work even after you get 'em off the showroom floor."

Andrea began laughing. "I've no idea what you just said."

"It's guy talk." He looked away and they sat in silence for a few moments. Finally, Jake said, "You know what? I liked it better when we were cousins."

"Me too."

She laid her hand in her lap, palm up. It looked like an offer he couldn't refuse. He reached for it and suddenly they were holding hands.

"I've heard that being married can be like being cousins," she said.

"I suppose part of marriage is like that. And part of it is probably like being roommates."

"Do you think I was unreasonable? About the milk, I mean," she asked.

"No, not at all. It was your milk. You paid for it. She had no right to drink it."

Andrea nodded. "Especially not out of the carton. I mean, does she think I want her germs?"

163

"Oh, I totally agree. Occasionally I drink milk out of the carton, but it's always milk I paid for."

"You have a right, then, to drink it anyway you want," she said.

"There's not a lot of different ways you can drink milk. Out of a glass, out of a cup, maybe a saucer, or out of the carton. That's about it."

"This is like talking to a roommate," she said.

"No kidding? Well, that's another one to add to our list."

"I have to admit, I'm a little confused right now," she said.

"How come?"

"I've always known I was going to get married in the temple. So things were really clear to me when you weren't a member of the Church."

Jake shrugged. "What can you do? These things happen—people get baptized and ruin all your plans."

"You've changed so much in the past few days."

"That's for sure. Right now I'm sinless. Jake Petricelli, the man with no sins. Right now, the slate is clean."

"Except for a little pride," she said.

"Pride?"

"Pride is a sin."

"You're kidding? Okay, maybe one."

She continued. "So I'm thinking, what if Jake keeps this up? What will he be like in a year? Will he have the Melchizedek Priesthood? Will he treat people with kindness? Will he be gentle and sensitive to others? Will he be worthy to go to the temple?"

"Not only that—I could be rich in a year."

"I don't care about that."

"Me either." He flinched. "That was a lie. Sorry. That's two."

"You want to put your arm around my shoulder?" she asked.

"Let's see. Like a cousin or a roommate?"

"I don't know. Try it and see."

He put his arm around her shoulder and drew her close. "This is very nice," he said. "Not really a cousin thing, and not a roommate thing either."

She turned to him. "What would you think if I told you I'm seriously considering accepting your proposal to get married in the temple in a year?"

"Really?"

"Really." She kissed him on the cheek. "Do you have a ring yet?"

This caught him completely off guard. He started rambling. "A ring? Do I have a ring? No, sorry. No ring. I could get one here, of course, but I'm sure I could get a better price in Seattle."

"Don't spend much on it, though, okay? The best gift I've ever received was you donating all that money to keep the swimming pool open."

Jake wiped his brow. "So, what are you saying, that you're thinking we might get married in a year?" he asked.

She nodded. "I know it seems like a long time, but we'll both be busy, so the time will go quickly. And then I'll be yours," she said with a smile.

"I can hardly wait," he said. But even as he said it, he knew he was lying.

And that bothered him tremendously.

* * * * *

Andrea came by for him early the next morning. He was packed and ready to go. She had brought some breakfast for them to share, and they ate it on the porch watching the morning come into existence. It was overcast, threatening to rain.

"I was thinking about us last night," she said, blushing as

she said it. "I'm definitely looking forward to being married to you."

Jake cleared his throat. "Yeah, that'll be nice," he said tentatively.

"Is something wrong?" she asked.

He looked away. "No. Are you kidding? What could be wrong?"

"Are you having second thoughts?"

"No, not at all."

"Then what's wrong?"

He walked off the porch and gazed at the lake and the mountains, trying to work up the courage to say it.

She came to him and looked up into his eyes. "Jake, please tell me what's wrong."

He turned to her and, almost apologetically, said, "I've been thinking about going on a mission."

"Really?" She let go of his arm, returned to the rocking chair, and began energetically rocking back and forth.

He stood there, apart from her, feeling foolish and afraid of what he'd done.

Finally he turned to face her. "So, what do you think?"

"I'm not sure you understand that you can't go on a mission until you've been a member for at least a year. And then, of course, you'd be gone for two years. So, actually, it'd be at least three years until you came back."

"I didn't know I'd have to wait a year."

"Three years is a long time. I hope you understand that I can't guarantee I'll be here for you when you get back."

"You'd marry someone else?" he asked.

"I'm just saying it could happen."

"Do you have anyone in mind?"

"No, of course not."

"Why wouldn't you wait for me then?"

"Three years? That's a lot to ask, Jake. Girls don't always wait. I see it happen all the time at Ricks."

I don't care what they say. There is an empty sea in this church, and this is it, he thought.

"This doesn't make sense," he said. "At first the main reason I learned about the Church was so you'd agree to marry me. That's all I wanted. Just you. I used to think that if I could have your love, I'd be the happiest man in the world."

"That's what I think now," she said softly.

"But when I was working on the mission cars, I felt really good, like this was something I could do to help Father in Heaven. I can fix cars, Andrea. I could do that on a mission."

"People don't go on missions to fix cars," she argued.

"I know, but it's something I know I can do. Besides, Elder Harbison said he thought I'd be a good missionary."

"This seems like a cruel joke." She looked at her watch and stood up. "It's time for you to go. Your train will be here in a few minutes."

They didn't say much on the way to the station. When they arrived, she stopped the car, and Jake said, "I don't know how to read you, Andrea. I thought you'd be happy about this."

"It's just that three years is a long time. I'm going to need some time to get used to the idea, that's all."

"Sure, me too."

The train was pulling into the yard. He grabbed his luggage from the backseat. "Thanks for the ride," he said.

She got out of the car, and he came around the car to give her a quick hug. "I'll call you tonight," he said, then waved and hurried to get on the train, leaving Andrea alone on the curb, feeling more alone than she had ever felt in her whole life.

11

It began raining shortly after Jake boarded the train. Because it was such a dreary day and so early in the morning, the dome car wasn't crowded. Jake found a seat and sat staring vacantly out the rain-spattered window.

He felt numb, and also betrayed. The only problem was he couldn't think who to blame. For one brief moment he'd had it all: faith, hope, and the girl he loved. And now, like a house of cards, it was all collapsing around him.

He had such an ache in his heart for Andrea, it was hard to think clearly. If he went on a mission, he might end up losing her. But if he didn't go, he'd feel as though he'd let himself and God down.

That was a new thought for him—that there was something he could do for God. All his life he had pictured God as some remote, angry presence, stern, most likely scowling at mankind, just waiting for somebody to mess up badly enough so he could send down punishment and wrath. But now Jake was beginning to think of him as a loving Father in Heaven. *What a big difference that makes,* he thought.

Do I believe this so much that I'm willing to risk losing Andrea in order to serve a mission? How can I go if she doesn't want me to?

He closed his eyes and tried to center on what was real

and what was not. *Did I become a Mormon just for Andrea? And if I did, then why let the Church come between us?*

He remembered how, when he first read about Alma's conversion, it seemed as though it had been written just for him, and how clean he'd felt after his baptism and confirmation. In a way it seemed almost too good to be true that God could forgive his sins, but in his heart he felt it had really happened.

He closed his eyes. In his mind he could hear Andrea singing: "I once was lost but now am found, was blind but now I see."

Jesus Christ has done so much for me, he thought. *He washed away my sins, took away my guilt, laid out a path for me to follow, gave me the Gift of the Holy Ghost, and let me know that I can help in His work.*

He retrieved Grampa's Book of Mormon from his bag and turned to a passage Elder Steiner had shown him; it was found in Third Nephi, chapter 27. They were the words of Jesus Christ, spoken after his resurrection:

Verily, verily, I say unto you, this is my gospel; and ye know the things that ye must do in my church; for the works which ye have seen me do that shall ye also do; for that which ye have seen me do even that shall ye do; Therefore, if ye do these things blessed are ye, for ye shall be lifted up at the last day.

Suddenly everything became clear to him. All his life he had lived just for himself. *It has always been what I want, what will make me happy,* he thought. The idea that we live to serve others had never occurred to him. But he could see it now. *I need to go on a mission. Not to fix cars, but to tell people about what's happened to me, so others can receive the same blessing.*

I'm going on a mission!

As he looked up from his reading and glanced out the train window, he saw Andrea, in her car, racing to keep up with the train, along a stretch of highway that paralleled the railroad track.

He stood up in the dome car and waved frantically. She saw him, waved, and nearly veered into an oncoming car.

Jake ran down the aisle looking for a conductor. Two cars later he ran into Montgomery. "Stop the train! I need to get off!"

"Why do you need to get off?"

Jake took him to a window. "See that car! I'm going to marry the girl who's driving it!"

"Well, isn't that wonderful!" Montgomery exclaimed.

"Can you stop the train?"

"I'm the conductor. I can do anything I want," Montgomery said with a big smile. "Excuse me. I'll be right back."

It seemed to take forever for the train to come to a complete stop. When it did, Montgomery gave Jake a thumbs up and sent him on his way.

"Send me an invitation to your wedding!" Montgomery shouted after him.

The tracks were now a quarter of a mile from the highway. Jake raced across a field of mountain flowers. When he came to a small brook, he tried to jump it, missed, and landed in the water feet first. With water squishing in his shoes, he continued up the hill toward the road above him.

Andrea was standing by the car waiting for him.

His right foot got stuck in some mud. When he tried to take another step, his foot came out of the shoe. He had to reach in with his hand and pull it out of the mud.

"I'm coming!" he shouted

"I want you to go on a mission, Jake! I'll wait for you for as long as it takes!" she shouted.

"That is so great, Andrea! Thank you! I love you!"

"I love you too!"

He struggled up the steep hillside, slippery with mud and

wet grass. Just before reaching the top, he lost his footing and slid backwards, all the way down again. He started laughing. "I'll make it this time!"

"If you don't, I'm coming down after you!"

"You know what?" he shouted. "I haven't done my ab exercises since I met you. Aren't you proud of me?"

She started laughing. "I am. You definitely are the man!"

"You still need a little work on that. It's *youda*," he puffed.

"Youda man!" she shouted.

"That's it! Now you've got it!" He started up the hill again.

"C'mon, Jake! You can do it!"

As he started to slip back down the hill again, he grabbed a tree stump and held on. "You know what? This is like the ultimate infomercial! I am so happy now!"

"I am too, but I'll be even happier if you ever make it up the hill."

Finally he made it to the top, grabbed both her hands, then, like kids doing "Ring around the Rosie," they spun around and around until they were both dizzy.

"How do you feel right now, at this very instant?" he asked.

She gave him a huge, two-dimple smile. "I feel great! How about you!"

He lifted both hands into the air and did a victory dance. "I feel like I've died and gone to Heaven!" he shouted.

They fell into each other's arms, saying over and over how much they loved each other, promising that they would wait no matter how long it took.

The train whistle sounded one long blast, and Montgomery waved to them both and stepped back on the train.

Soon the train was gone from sight. But they didn't care anymore. They knew where they were going, and how to get there.

171